Epes S

The New American Fourth Reader

Anatiposi

Epes Sargent, Amasa May

The New American Fourth Reader

Reprint of the original, first published in 1871.

1st Edition 2023 | ISBN: 978-3-38211-484-8

Anatiposi Verlag is an imprint of Outlook Verlagsgesellschaft mbH.

Verlag (Publisher): Outlook Verlag GmbH, Zeilweg 44, 60439 Frankfurt, Deutschland
Vertretungsberechtigt (Authorized to represent): E. Roepke, Zeilweg 44, 60439 Frankfurt, Deutschland
Druck (Print): Books on Demand GmbH, In de Tarpen 42, 22848 Norderstedt, Deutschland

E. H. BUTLER & CO.'S NEW AMERICAN SERIES.

THE NEW AMERICAN FOURTH READER,

BY EPES SARGENT AND AMASA MAY.

PHILADELPHIA:
J. H. BUTLER & CO.

PREFACE.

In the advertisement of a series of Readers prepared by one of the present editors seventeen years ago, he remarked: "Although the editor has been more solicitous to offer what is suitable than what is novel, it will be found that more than two-thirds of this collection is composed of pieces that have a place in no other Readers."

Unfortunately, he cannot say this of that former collection *now;* for, in some series of Readers widely circulated in the United States, the compilers have availed themselves of his sedulous labors to an extent of which he might justly complain, since they have appropriated not only his new and carefully-adapted selections, but a number of pieces *wholly original and protected by copyright,* though published either without his name or under the assumed names of Osborne, Vinet, etc. Two of these pieces we have here taken the liberty to reclaim, with such alterations as the author has chosen to make.

Believing that quality and adaptedness are more to be considered in a reading-book than a superfluity of matter, it has been our purpose to make a CHEAP, COMPACT AND SKILLFULLY-GRADUATED SERIES, containing not one piece that a teacher of sound literary taste would skip on account of demerits in style or sense. The quantity of bad verse in some popular reading-books is too frequently a trial to both teacher and pupil.

We have been careful, too, to give, in the present volume, such a variety that the declamatory and the colloquial, the emotional and the unimpassioned forms of speech should all be represented in fair proportions.

Exercises and hints of a purely practical nature will be found in the Introduction. Every teacher should master them.

To the original pictorial illustrations of this series, so creditable to American art, we call attention with especial satisfaction.

WESTCOTT & THOMSON, Stereotypers, Philada. SHERMAN & CO., Printers, Philada.

TABLE OF CONTENTS

INTRODUCTION.

LESSONS IN PROSE.

LESSONS IN VERSE.

DIALOGUES.

INTRODUCTION.

Elementary Sounds.—An Elementary Sound is one which cannot be divided into two or more unlike sounds. For instance, the **a** in *far* is elementary, but the **i** in *ride* is compounded of **a** in *far* and **e** in *me*, closely joined in the utterance, thus: **a-e** = **i** long.

The Elementary Sounds of the English language do not properly exceed thirty-four. Owing to the defects of our alphabet, to represent all these sounds we have only twenty-six letters, and some of these are of no real service: **c**, for example, could be expressed by **s** or **k** (as in *city*, *can*); **q** by **kw**, and **x** by **ks** or **gz**.

In the absence of single letters as signs for certain Elementary Sounds, we have to use two letters; as for **ng** in *thing*; **sh** in *shine*; **th** in *thin* and *thine*. Bear in mind that different letters are often used to express the same sound, as in *care* and *there*, and sometimes two, three or four letters are used to express the sound of one. Thus, the word *awe* simply expresses the sound of **a** in *fall*; **ea** in *great*, the sound of **a** in *fate*; **eau** in *beauty*, the sound of **u** in *mute*; **augh** in *slaughter*, the sound of **a** in *fall*.

Two letters used together to denote one sound are called a *digraph*; thus, in the word *ring*, **n** and **g** form a digraph.

When two vowels unite to form a syllable, they are called a *diphthong*, as in *aid*, *mean*, *hoist*. When three vowels so unite, they are called a *triphthong*, as in *beauty*, *view*.

The Elementary Sounds are **a** in *far*, **a** in *fat*, **a** in *fate*, **a** in *fall*; **e** in *me*, **e** in *met*; **i** in *fit*; **o** in *note*, **o** in *not*; **u** in *bull*; **oo** in *cool*; **u** in *but*; **w** in *wet*; **y** in *yet*; **h** in *hot*; **ng** in *king*; **m** in *man*; **n** in *not*; **l** in *let*; **r** in *run*; **p** in *pan* and **b** in *bag*; **f** in *fan* and **v** in *van*; **th** in *thin* and **th** in *thine*; **t** in *tin* and **d** in *din*; **k** in *kind* and **g** in *gun*; **s** in *sin* and **z** in *zeal*; **sh** in *shine* and **z** in *azure*.

Besides these there are four Compound Vowel Sounds sometimes classed with the Elementary; namely, long **i** in *pine*, long **u** in *cube*, **ou** in *house*, **oi** in *voice*; and two Compound Consonant Sounds, namely, **ch** in *chest*, **j** in *jest*.

Vowels and Consonants.—A Consonant is an element of speech formed by means of a complete or partial closing of the vocal tube; and being itself an obscure sound, it generally requires the help of a vowel for its intelligible utterance. A Vowel can be uttered without a closing of the vocal tube, and without the aid of any other sound. The vowels are **a**, **e**, **i**, **o**, **u**, and sometimes **w** and **y**.

One Consonant Sound is said to be *cognate* to another when it is related or allied to it; as **p** to **b**, **f** to **v**, **th** in *thin* to **th** in *thine;* **t** to **d**, **k** to **g** hard (as in *gun*), **s** to **z**, **sh** in *shine* to **z** in *azure.* Of these, **p**, **f**, **th** in *thin*, **t**, **k**, **s** and **sh** are said to be Aspirate; the others, Vocal.

The **a** in *ask* and the **a** in *care* are not classed among the Elementary Sounds, as they are regarded generally as mere modifications of the sounds of **a** in **at** and **a** in *fate.* Examples in which they occur will be found in the Exercises on the Vowel Sounds.

Phonic Analysis.—The alphabetic names of letters being no true guides to their sounds when formed into words, it is desirable to give the actual sounds independently, and this process is called Phonic Analysis, the word *phonic* being derived from the Greek *pho'ne*, a sound.

In this exercise it is obvious that no heed is to be taken of silent letters. Thus, the word *water* has the same number of sounds as *daughter*.

Print some simple word on the blackboard and explain its Elementary Sounds. Take, for example, the word *map*, in which there are as many sounds as there are letters: **m**, short **a**, and **p**:

Map m-m-m a-a-a p-p-p map.

After the separate sounds of this word are perfectly understood, select one with a new element in it, and exercise pupils on that; first calling on them to say whether it has as many sounds as it has letters.

Man m-m-m a-a-a n-n-n man.

Proceed now to illustrate the fact that, owing to the poverty of our alphabet and the capricious irregularities in our modes of forming words by letters, the same letter, a, is used for a variety of sounds. This may be shown in *make, car, fall,* etc. Show that one device for helping us out has been to attach a silent vowel-letter (as in *make* = m-a-k) to indicate the long sound of a in a large class of words.

Make m-m-m a-a-a k-k-k make.

In the word *car* we have the sounds of k, a in *father* and smooth or untrilled r.

Car k-k-k a-a-a r-r-r car.

Here it may be illustrated that the presence of r should give a slight, but not a too formal, difference to our enunciation of such words as *alms* and *arms, balm* and *farm.*

In the word *thaw* there are only two Elementary Sounds, namely, aspirate th and the sound of a in *fall.* Call upon pupils to designate the Elementary Sounds in the following words: *trough* (t r o f), *enough, physic, child, shine, thin, thine, sleigh, calf, autumn, awe, aught, height, freight, prove, laugh, sphere,* etc.

In Phonic Spelling the division of syllables may be marked by pauses instead of repetitions. If the teacher finds it difficult to discover and produce the true sounds of a word, let him refer to the dictionary, and then pronounce the sounds deliberately and distinctly, so that they may separately strike the ear; as, for example, in the word *poison = p-oi-s-n.*

In Syllabic Analysis first pronounce the whole word, then repeat it with the exception of the first syllable, then with the exception of the second, etc., until the last syllable; as, *al-pha-bet-ic, pha-bet-ic, bet-ic, ic.* To analyze by sound, pronounce the whole word, and repeat it with the exception of the first sound, then with the exception of the second, and so on till only one sound remains.

Exercises in Vowel Sounds.

a, as in *far*.—Father, *arm*, *are*, *aunt*, *balm*, *bath*, *calf*, *calm*, *daunt*, draught (draft), *guard*, *haunt*, *hearth*, *jaundice*, *lath*, *laugh*, *launch*, *laundry*, *path*, *psalm*, *qualm*, *salve*, *saunter*, *sergeant*, *taunt*.

a, short, as in *hat*.—*Apt*, *acrid*, *catch*, *clamber*, *gas*, *gather*, *matin*, *national*, *panic*, *plaid*, *raillery*, *rather*, *rational*, *tapestry*, *tarry*, *tassel*.

a, long, as in *hate*.—*Ale*, *angel*, *aye*, *bait*, *blazon*, *cambric*, *campaign*, *chaste*, *chasten*, *convey*, *deign*, *estrange*, *feign*, *gauge*, *great*, *heinous*, *inveigh*, *matron*, *neighbor*, *obey*, *placable*, *sleigh*, *steak*, *straight*, *stranger*, *weigh*.

a, broad, as in *fall*; the equivalent of *o* in *nor*.—*All*, *alter*, *auction*, *aught*, *balk*, *balsam*, *broad*, *brought*, *calk*, *caught*, *falcon*, *falchion*, *fawn*, *forlorn*, *halt*, *orb*, *palsy*, *paltry*, *sward*, *saucy*, *swart*, *thought*, *walnut*, *wampum*.

a, as in *ask* (called by some intermediate *a*; pronounced by some like *a* in *dare*; by some like *a* in *far*; by some like *a* in *hat*).—*Basket*, *branch*, *clasp*, *class*, *dance*, *flask*, *grass*, *mask*, *mastiff*, *past*, *plaster*, *vast*.

e, long, as in *me*.—*Brief*, *caprice*, *Cæsar*, *cede*, *dear*, *deceit*, *demon*, *e'en*, *either* (also pronounced īther), *fatigue*, *field*, *fiend*, *grieve*, *inveigle*, *key*, *machine*, *people*, *quay* (ke), *ravine*, *receipt*, *seize*, *siege*, *tea*.

e, short, as in *met*.—*Bed*, *again*, *against*, *any*, *bestial*, *bread*, *breakfast*, *cellar*, *cleanse*, *deaf*, *engine*, *erring*, *friend*, *get*, *guess*, *heifer*, *kettle*, *leant*, *leopard*, *many*, *peasant*, *preface*, *ready*, *said*, *says*, *sterile*, *tepid*, *very*, *yet*, *zealot*.

e, as in *her*.—*Herd*, *fern*, *fervid*, *bird*, *pearl*, *learn*, *earl*, *earth*, *heard*, *mercy*, *mirth*, *girl*, *person*, *term*, *stern*, *worm*, *word*, *worth*, *worse*, *nurse*, *pert*, *rehearse*, *first*, *nurst*, *worst*, *burst*, *furl*, *curl*, *world*. (Avoid the tendency to slight the sound of untrilled *r* in this class of words.)

i, short, as in *hit*.—*Bid*, *been*, *biscuit*, *breeches*, *build*, *busy*, *conduit*, *England*, *feminine*, *forfeit*, *give*, *juvenile*, *livelong*, *lyric*, *mirror*, *guilt*, *sieve*, *spirit*, *synod*, *tribune*, *typify*, *vineyard*, *witty*, *women*, *withe* (the *th* aspirate, as in hath).

i, long, as in *find*.—*Apply*, *ally*, *bind*, *blight*, *buy*, *child*, *eye*, *fly*, *guide*, *guile*, *height* or *hight*, *indict*, *isle*, *oblige*, *rye*, *sigh*, *sky*, *satiety*, *sinecure*, *tiny*.

o, long, as in note.—Boat, beau, bolster, bone, both, bowl, bowsprit, brooch, cocoa, dotard, dough, droll, engross, fellow, foe, knoll, loth, most, only, oral, patrol′, scroll, sew, strew, sloth, soap, stone, soul, toad, troll, trow, whole, woe.

o, short, as in got.—Blot, dross, florid, forehead, gloss, grovel, hovel, jocund, knowledge, moth, product, quality, sorry, swamp, squadron, trode, wan, was, watch.

u, as in full; the equivalent of short *oo*, as in book.—Bush, butcher, could, cuckoo, cushion, hook, look, pull, pulley, pulpit, push, put, should, wolf, woolen or woollen, woman, wood, would.

oo, long, as in cool.—Bloom, balloon, bruise, brutal, canoe, croup, cruise, do, fruit, group, lose, moon, move, prove, prudent, prune, rheum, rule, shoe, surtout, true, two, uncouth, who.

u, short, as in but.—Cut, above, among, blood, brother, color, comely, cousin, does, done, dost, doth, double, dove, enough, flood, flourish, front, hurry, joust, money, none, nothing, some, tongue, young.

u, long, as in mute (sometimes called diphthongal *u*, and having a sound of initial *y*).—Cube, dew, due, feud, knew, neutral, new, reduce, stew, student, stupid, tube, Tuesday, tumid, tutor, view.

ou, as in house.—Brow, cloud, down, dowry, cow, crowd, doubt, drought, noun, now, out, powder, pronounce, town, trout, vow.

oi, as in voice.—Avoid, boil, broil, choice, coin, coy, foible, hoist, join, joist, loin, loiter, oil, oyster, point, poise, rejoice, soil, spoil, toil, voyage.

Long Vowels Modified by r.—When long *a* occurs before *r* in the same syllable, as in bare, care, etc., the sound is so modified as to conform to that of the first *e* in there, where, etc. Long *o* is also modified by *r*, as in bore, more.

a, as in care.—Bare, bear, chary, daring, heir, impair, pare, parent, rare, share, snare, stair, tear, wear.

o, as in more.—Adore, afford, bore, core, door, floor, four, lore, mourn, pork, portal.

Unaccented Vowel Sounds.—A feeble enunciation of the vowel sounds in unaccented syllables is a common fault, but a precision leading to stiffness in utterance should be avoided. In words ending in unaccented *-ary*, *-ery*, *-ory*, the vowel before *r* is usually short, and should be sounded accordingly, though without stress. The same may be said of endings in *-able*, as, valu*a*ble. In a large class of words, long *a* in unaccented syllables (as in vill*a*ge, desper*a*te, moun*tai*n) should lose so much stress as to approach the sound of short *i*. But in verbs (as regul*a*te) and in certain nouns (as candid*a*te) long *a*, though unaccented, has its regular sound. The following sentence shows the difference in the sound of long *a* unaccented in a verb and in an adjective: "Intimāte the fact to your intim*a*te friend."

In unaccented syllables the short sounds of *a* and *e* (as in dorm*a*nt, ard*e*nt) are relatively fainter than in accented syllables, but they should not degenerate into the sounds of *ŭ* or ĭ.

Short *a* unaccented when initial (as in *a*live) or coming after a consonant (as in c*a*ress) should have the sound it has in its easy utterance in "Once *a* week." Unaccented *a* final or before *r*, as in comm*a*, ced*a*r, etc., also has this sound.

The unaccented vowel in *evil, drivel*, etc. (pronounced *ev'l, driv'l*), is unsounded, but in many other words it is sounded; as, anv*i*l, chap*e*l, fin*a*l, med*a*l, mod*e*l, parc*e*l, penc*i*l, rev*e*l.

Short *e* or *i* unaccented before *n* should be sounded in the following words: chick*e*n, childr*e*n, kitch*e*n, lin*e*n, slov*e*n, sudd*e*n, Lat*i*n, mat*i*n, sat*i*n, etc., but in many other words it should be silent; as, dozen, driven, even, golden, heaven, kitten, often, open, seven, soften, spoken, basin, cousin, raisin, etc.

Short *o* unaccented is heard without stress in the following words: comm*o*n, dem*o*n, her*o*n, serm*o*n, summ*o*n, ten*o*n; but in the following the *o* should be unsounded: bacon, beacon, deacon, pardon, person, poison, reason, treason, weapon, etc.

The sound of long *o* unaccented, as in fell*ow*, wid*ow*, should not be corrupted into the sound of *er*.

Long, diphthongal *u* (as in m*u*te) is generally heard pure when it ends or forms a syllable (unless preceded by the sound of *r*) either immediately before or after the accent; as m*u*tation, *u*nite, ed*u*cate, etc. But in certain unaccented terminations in *-ure* (as in creat*ure*, nat*ure*, etc.) long *u*, while preserving its *y* element, loses a little of its sound of long *oo*, so that these words are pronounced nearly as if creat'*yŭr*, nat'*yŭr*.

Exercises in Consonant Sounds.

Let the reader first pronounce the representative sound by itself, giving, if practicable, not merely its alphabetic name, but its true phonic quality, and then apply it to the words offered as examples.

b, vocal, as in *barb*.—*B*ab*b*le, *b*oo*b*y, *b*ul*b*, ca*b*, cri*b*, e*bb*, im*b*i*b*e, lo*bb*y, mo*b*, ra*b*id, ri*b*, sta*b*, we*b*.

ch, aspirate, as in *church*.—*Ch*afe, *ch*amber, *ch*eap, di*tch*, ha*tch*, mar*ch*ing, mil*ch*, su*ch*, tou*ch*, whi*ch*.

d, vocal, as in *did*.—*D*egra*d*e, e*dd*y, fa*d*e, gi*dd*y, ho*d*, la*d*, mo*d*e, no*d*, pa*dd*e*d*, we*dd*e*d*.

f, aspirate, as in *fife*.—*F*ar, *f*ĕo*ff*, *f*ive, *f*ew, lau*gh*, em*ph*asis, o*ff*, o*f*ten, nym*ph*, *ph*antom, *ph*easant, pro*ph*et, *ph*ysic, rou*gh*, sa*pph*ire, so*f*ten, sou*gh*, s*ph*ere, tou*gh*.

g, vocal, as in *gag*.—Co*g*nate, *gh*ost, e*gg*, fo*g*, *G*ertrude, *g*ibber, *g*i*gg*le, *g*imp, *g*uile, lo*g*, physio*g*nomy, pla*gue*, ra*g*, va*gue*.

h, as in *hail*.—*H*igh, *h*ymn, ex*h*aust, ex*h*ibit, ex*h*ort, in*h*ale, per*h*aps, re*h*earse, *wh*om, with*h*old.

j, vocal, as in *jar*.—A*g*e, *g*elatin, *g*em, *g*erund, *g*ibbet, *g*ibe, *g*iblet, *g*ipsy, *g*ist, *g*in, hu*g*e, *j*ar, *j*elly, *j*ib, lo*dg*e, pa*g*e, sol*d*ier, wa*g*er.

k, aspirate, as in *kirk*.—A*ch*e, ar*ch*itect, ar*k*, *c*ape, con*ch*, co*q*uette, disti*ch*, e*ch*o, ep'o*ch*, fla*c*cid, *k*in, lo*ch*, ta*lk*, wa*lk*.

l, as in *lily*.—Ba*ll*, ce*ll*ar, ev*il*, flanne*l*, i*ll*y, ki*ln*, *l*ake, *l*o*ll*, *l*ove*l*y, *l*u*ll*, me*ll*ow, si*ll*y, tit*le*, trave*l*, weas*el*, woo*ll*y.

m, as in *maim*.—Cli*m*b, colu*mn*, conde*mn*, da*m*e, dra*chm*, el*m*, hy*mn*, la*mb*, li*mn*, li*m*'ner, *m*i*m*e, *m*ur*m*ur.

n, as in *nun*.—Basi*n*, co*n*dig*n*, cousi*n*, eve*n*, *gn*at, *gn*aw, i*nn*, *kn*eel, *kn*ow*n*, Lati*n*, mali*gn*, *n*ou*n*, slove*n*, ta*nn*i*n*.

ng, as in ri*ng*.—Acti*ng*, a*n*chor, a*n*ger, ba*n*k, co*n*gress, co*n*quest, fi*n*ger, ga*ng*, ly*n*x, nothi*ng*, ra*n*k, si*ng*er, si*n*k, unth*in*king, you*n*ger.

p, aspirate, as in *pipe*.—A*p*t, *p*a*p*, *p*om*p*, *p*o*p*ulous, *p*u*pp*et, *p*u*p*il, shar*p*, sli*pp*er, stee*p*, vam*p*.

r, rough or trilled (beginning a word or syllable with or without a consonant element).—A*r*ound, cont*r*a*r*y, lib*r*a*r*y, p*r*ay, *r*are, *rh*ubarb, *wr*ap.

r, smooth or untrilled (occurring as the last consonant, or last but one or two, in a syllable or word. This sound should be so far heard that, for example, *form* is not converted into *fawm*).—Abhor, bar*e*, ene*r*gy, expi*r*e, e*rr*, fi*r*, hi*r*e, me*r*cy, mo*r*tgage, mu*r*mu*r*ing, no*r*, pa*r*don, to*r*po*r*, wo*r*d.

s, aspirate, as in *s*ad.—Cha*s*ten, de*s*ign, de*s*i*s*t*s*, do*s*e, ho*s*t*s*, ma*ss*, p*s*alm, *s*cene, *sch*ism, va*c*cinate, verbo*s*e.

sh, aspirate, as in *sh*y.—*Ch*agrin, *ch*aise, *ch*arade, *ch*arlatan, *ch*icane, *ch*ivalry, cons*ciou*s, diver*si*on, ma*ch*ine, mar*sh*, *sh*all, *sh*riek, *sh*rill, *sh*rub, spe*ci*al, *s*ugar, *s*ure, ver*si*on.

t, aspirate, as in *t*en*t*.—As*th*ma, bri*t*tle, dance*d*, deb*t*, drou*ght*, flourishe*d*, indic*t*, *phth*isic, sub*t*le, ta*tt*er, *t*augh*t*, *th*yme, vic*t*ual, wrecke*d*, yach*t*.

th, aspirate, as in *th*in.—Betrŏ*th*ed, brea*th*, eigh*th*, oa*th*, mou*th*, six*th*, *th*ank, tru*th*, tru*th*s, twelf*th*, wi*th*e.

th, vocal, as in *th*ine.—Ba*th*e, ba*th*s, benea*th*, bli*th*e, boo*th*, boo*th*s, mou*th* (when a verb), mou*th*s, oa*th*s, pa*th*s, *th*ere, *th*i*th*er, underne*ath*, unshea*th*e, whi*th*er, wi*th*, wi*th*al, wi*th*er, wi*th*hold, wi*th*-stand.

v, vocal, as in *v*al*v*e.—A*v*arice, bra*v*e, ner*v*e, ne*ph*ew, o*f*, Ste*ph*en, *v*i*v*id, *v*oid, *v*oti*v*e, wea*v*e.

w, as in *w*ill (in *one*, *once*, the *o* stands for the sound of *u* short as well as *w*).—Ch*o*ir (k*w*ĭr), c*u*irass (k*w*e-ras′), *o*nce, *o*ne, q*u*ake, s*u*ite (s*w*ēt), s*w*ear, *w*ay*w*ard, *w*ine, *w*orm*w*ood.

wh, aspirate, as in *wh*it.—*Wh*ale, *wh*at, *wh*ere, *wh*en, *wh*ether, *wh*ile, *wh*irl, *wh*ist, *wh*isper, *wh*ite, *wh*ose.

x, aspirate, like *ks*, as in bo*x*.—E*x*cept, e*x*ecute, e*x*hume, com-ple*x*ion, ne*x*t, se*x*ton, ta*x*es, te*x*t.

x, vocal, like *gz*, as in e*x*ert.—E*x*act, e*x*alt, e*x*amine, e*x*ample, e*x*empt, e*x*hale, e*x*otic, an*x*iety.

y, as in *y*et.—Fil*i*al, pon*i*ard, rebell*i*on, *y*awn, *y*ield, *y*on, *y*onder, *y*ore, *y*outh.

z, vocal, as in *z*eal.—A*s*, bar*s*, cave*s*, di*s*join, di*s*mal, ha*s*, hu*ss*ar*s*, i*s*, ma*z*e, na*s*al, ob*s*erve*s*, po*s*sess, sci*ss*or*s*, sea*s*, suffu*s*e, wa*s*, *X*erxe*s*.

z, vocal, like *zh*, as in a*z*ure.—Adhe*s*ion, colli*s*ion, fu*s*ion, gla*z*ier, lei*s*ure, o*s*ier, plea*s*ure, trea*s*ure, vi*s*ion.

Aspirate Consonant Sounds.—Shape, if, laugh, path, breath, breaths, pith, health, strength, apt, miss, whip, ax, puff'd, stamp'd, ink'd, waltz, inch, milch, sing'st, gulfs, expects, next, wastes, desks, fifths, twelfths, milk'st, flinch'd, attempt'st, texts, sixths, betrŏth'd, truths.

Vocal Consonant Sounds.—Babe, trade, egg, leave, of, bathe, breathe, with, beneath, underneath, ease, as, buzz, ale, isle am, tongue, bulb, build, delve, aims, comes, bronze, pangs, stabb'd, cabs, odds, liv'd, grazed, loaves, bathes, helm, film, lands, change, delv'd, shelves, judg'd, besieg'd, bronz'd.

Miscellaneous Combinations.—Nymphs, triumph'd, thump'st, prompts, wince, avalanche, plinth, taunt'st, filch'd, hold'st, gulfs, mulcts, halt'st, hark'dst, warm'd'st, harp'dst, rippl'st, troubl'st, trifl'dst, laugh'st, waft'st, settl'd, settl'dst, hard'n'dst, did'st, digg'st, mask'st, clasps, insists, driv'l, driv'l'st, driv'l'dst, muzzl'dst, chasm, chasms, pris'n, reas'n'd, reas'n'dst, reas'nst, shrink, shroud, push'd, hush'd, fetch'd, scratch'd, besieg'd.

Pronunciation.—Among the most common errors is the omission of one or more elements in a word; as, *sen's* for sends, *fac's* for facts, *promp's* for prompts, *sof'ly* for softly, *hist'ry* for history, etc. Do not substitute one sound for another, as in saying *set* for sit, *jest* for just, *yit* for yet, *sullar* for cellar, *crik* for creek, *srill* for shrill, *wen* for when, *mornin'* for morning, *feller* for fellow, *heerd* for heard, *herth* for hearth (the *ea* as in h*ea*rt), etc.

Of words ending in *-el, -en, -il, -in* or *-on*, those in which the unaccented vowel ought to be sounded, as in chick*en*, civ*il*, tend*on*, etc., should be discriminated from those in which it ought to be silent, as in *often* (of'n), *heaven* (hev'n), *even* (ev'n), *cousin* (kuz'n), etc.

More Common Errors.—Do not interpose a vowel sound between *l* or *s* and *m* in such words as *elm, helm, chasm*, etc., as if they were *elum*, etc.

Smooth *r* should not be trilled, as in saying *for-rm* for form, nor should it be suppressed, as in saying *faw* for for, *nus* for nurse, *fust* for first, *wus* for worse, nor sounded where it does not properly belong, as in saying *lawr* for law. Words in which the digraph *th* has its aspirate sound, as in *thin*, should be discriminated from those where it has its vocal sound, as in brea*th*e, benea*th*, wi*th*, etc. Do not interpose the sound of *e* long after the consonants *k* and *g* hard preceding the sound of *i*, as if *kind* were *ke-ind*, or *guide, gee-ide*. Do not pervert the sound of *ou* (as in bound, now) into *eeow* or *aow*, as if *cow* were *kaow* and *county, kaounty*. The pure sound of *oi* must not be changed into long *i*, as if *joint* were *jint*.

When a word ends with *s* and the next word begins with *s*, the sounds must be distinctly separated; as, "The hosts . . . still fought;" "the mists . . . seem gathering." Do not pervert the sound of *aw* into *or;* do not say *droring* for *drawing*.

Accent.—By Accent we mean the stress of the voice on a certain syllable of a word of more than one syllable. This stress may be indicated to the eye by the acute accent, thus: ex′ple-tive, mu-se′um, con-tra-dict′. Several words which are spelled alike, as nouns or adjectives and verbs, are distinguished, when spoken, by a difference of accent; as, *a* reb′el, *to* re-bel′; *an* in′sult, *to* in-sult′; *a* per′fume, *to* per-fume′; fre′-quent, *to* fre-quent′.

Emphasis.—The sense of a sentence often depends on the right placing of the emphasis. Thus in the question, "Did you give him a ripe orange?" the direct meaning may be taken in seven different ways, according as the emphasis is laid on the seven words separately. See page 120.

Pause.—There are two kinds of pauses, namely, Grammatical and Rhetorical pauses. Grammatical pauses are denoted by the marks of punctuation, as the comma, semicolon, colon, period, etc., but ordinary punctuation is no guide for oratorical pausing. Many more pauses than are indicated to the eye ought to be observed, and will be if attention is given to the sense or the emotional quality of what is read.

In the following passages the dash indicates the division of the sentence at which the longest pause may be made. The points or dotted places indicate that an inferior momentary pause may take place:

"I am persuaded . . . that neither death nor life . . . nor angels . . nor principalities . . nor powers . . . nor things present . . . nor things to come . . . nor height . . . nor depth . . . nor any other creature—shall be able to separate us . . . from the love of God."

"We make provision for this life . . . as though it were never to have an end—and for the other life . . . as though it were never to have a beginning."

Inflections.—When you utter the word "Come!" in an entreating sense, the tone is quite different from that which you would give to the word "Go!" uttered sternly. These different tones are called *inflections of the voice*, and, in the foregoing examples, the word "Come" has the *Rising* inflection and the word "Go" the *Falling*. These inflections naturally occur, with more or less force, in reading as well as in our common conversation.

In counting one, two, three, etc., up to twelve, we give the rising inflection to every number till we come to the last, and to that we give the falling. In the question, "Did you say one?" uttered in an ordinary tone of inquiry, the word *one* takes the Rising inflection. In the question, "When did I say one?" uttered without some modifying emotion, the last word takes the Falling inflection.

The upward or Rising inflection is usually indicated by an acute accent (/), and the downward or Falling inflection by the grave accent (\). The Rising inflection is that tone which we give to what is incomplete or suspended; as, "Did he say No′?" It is the tone of doubt or entreaty. The Falling inflection is the tone of completeness and command.

Indirect questions, or those commencing with an adverb or pronoun, and which cannot be grammatically answered by a simple *yes* or *no*, generally take the Falling inflection, and so do the answers to such questions; as, "Where is he going‵?" —"I don't know‵."

When exclamatory sentences become questions, or are expressive of tender emotions, they usually take the Rising inflection; as, "They planted by your care′?" "O‵! my son Absalom′!" But passion and emphasis break through all the rules that can be laid down for inflection. When the indirect question is not understood, and a repetition is required, it takes the Rising inflection; as. "Whose book is it‵?" "Mine‵." "Whose did you say′?"

Language of deep emotion, of authority, surprise, denunciation or terror, generally takes the Falling inflection; as, "Me miserable\!" "What a piece of work is a man\!" Words and clauses connected by the disjunctive *or* generally require the Rising inflection before and the Falling after it; as, "Shall we go′ or stay\?"

The Circumflex is a combination of the two inflections. The Falling, followed by the Rising, may be indicated to the eye thus (⌄); the Rising, followed by the Falling, thus (^). These tones are used in the language of irony and derision or of contrast. We have examples of both in the following:

"Hear him, my lord; he is wondrous cǒndescênding."

Monotone.—When no inflection is used, a *monotone* or sameness of tone is produced. This, though generally to be avoided, is sometimes appropriate and impressive, especially in sublime or solemn passages.

Parenthesis.—Parenthetical sentences require the tone to be somewhat monotonous, and the rate of utterance rather more rapid than in the principal sentence. The parenthesis also requires a slight pause both before and after it; as, "He said (and I believed him) the enemy were ten thousand strong." See page 122.

Vocal Training.

The voice should be well exercised on the Elementary Sounds, for, when pronounced singly, these will receive a concentration of effort, the habit of which will ensure distinctness and force in the compounds of speech.

Exercise of the Breath.—The management of the breath in speaking can be best learned from the individual's own practice. It is a good exercise for him to repeat the cardinal numbers, one, two, three, etc., rapidly up to twenty, first inhaling a full breath. He may, by practice, make his breath hold out till he reaches forty and more, enunciating every syllable distinctly.

A good exercise in breathing may be had by noting the number of seconds required to fill the lungs by slow inhalation, and then by slow exhalation; also by noting how many syllables may be uttered without a fresh supply of breath.

Gymnastic Aids.—Preliminary muscular actions are a good preparation for vocal effort, and gymnastic or calisthenic exercises, judiciously regulated, are important aids in the development of the voice.

Position of the Body.—Teachers should be especially careful to demand of the pupil a proper position and carriage of the body. In reading, the attitude should be erect, without stiffness, and the chest well expanded. A constrained or a lounging posture is fatal to a free and spirited use of the voice. Let the teacher see that even in his manner of holding the book the pupil conforms to the rules of grace and ease.

Management of Voice.—The medium quality of every person's voice is his common conversational key, which is always more easy and graceful than any other. What are generally called "reading tones," and which are mostly *higher* than the natural key pitch, should be for the most part avoided. The more simple and natural our style, the more effective it must always be to the ears of good judges.

Expressive Delivery.—Having acquired that control over the vocal organs which will render the effort of speech the easiest to ourselves and the most agreeable to others, we must learn to convey meaning and emotion by the proper use of emphasis, and by tones in sympathy with the character of the words, the language and the thought.

To attain to a pathetic eloquence, the pupil must realize the significance of *words*. Who, in uttering the following words,

Slow, rapid, strength, weakness, harsh, smooth, torturing, pleasing, exasperating, tranquilizing, crumble, stumble, crash, flash, luminous, obscure, split, snap, crackle, purling, rustling, etc., does not feel in some degree the ideas they impart? How much stronger, then, must be the effect when such expressive words are introduced by the great orator or poet into eloquent or descriptive speech!

Capabilities of the Voice.—So capable of variety is the human voice that, like a well-tuned instrument, it faithfully responds to every impulse of the emotions. In joy it is clear, animated and melodious; in grief it is soft, plaintive and interrupted; in anger it is harsh and hurrying, and may be low or loud according to the circumstances; in fear it is slow, suppressed and hesitating. Tender and flowing in persuasion, it is stern and awful in threatening, slow in conjecture and firm in assertion. In applause it expands, in reproach it contracts. It warbles in pleasure, swells in courage, storms in rage and thunders in command.

Force.—No direction can be given for the proper employment of the various degrees of Force: their use is dependent on the meaning of the words spoken, the situation of the supposed speaker, the relative positions and distances of the speaker and hearer, and, principally, on taste and judgment.

Compass.—For acquiring extent of tone, the best method is for the pupil to practice his voice by raising it to its utmost extent in full tones, and then by semi-tones; after that let him be taught to fall, by just progression, to its lowest pitch.

For instance, in the passage, "Hear me, for I *will* speak." let the first word *hear* be uttered in the lowest chest tone that you can render articulate. Speak the whole sentence in that middle range which is only a small degree above a whisper. The next time pronounce the word *hear* a full note higher than the former, and the whole sentence accordingly. Proceed in this manner till you reach the highest note, and then descend from the highest to the lowest.

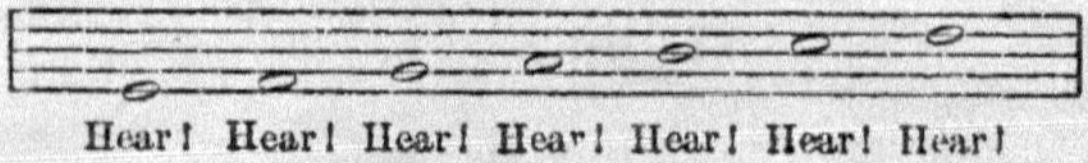

THE NEW AMERICAN FOURTH READER

LESSON I.

BULK, size; mass.
EF'FORT, trial; endeavor.
FI'BER or FI'BRE, any fine, slender thread; a filament.
GUESS, to suppose.
SHAFT, a stem; a trunk.
STATE'LY, grand; lofty.
STU-PEN'DOUS, wonderful; vast.

THE TREE THAT WAS ONCE LITTLE.

1. EDWIN and his sister, being in California with their father, went to look at one of the great trees that excite so much wonder. This tree was called

The Giant, and its bark alone was two feet thick. If the trunk had been cut off smoothly near its base, fifty horses could easily have stood on it together, or a number of large tents could have been pitched there.

2. "How old do you think this tree is?" asked Edwin. "It must be at least two thousand years old," said his father. "By counting the circles in its woody fiber we might guess its age. From a little seed no bigger than a pea this huge tree has grown. Little by little it has taken to itself bulk and form; and much of its bulk must have been got from the air alone.

3. "Learn from this, my children, what may be done in our human efforts if we will be but content to grow in knowledge little by little. You tell me now that you cannot understand many things in your lessons, that you do not know the meaning of many words you meet with, and that when you see how much there is to learn you almost despair.

4. "Little by little, if you will but try, you will grow to understand what now seems so difficult. One new word a day is something gained, but you can do better than that. This stupendous tree was once a slender little shoot. It had the winds and storms to strive against, year after year, until it now stands a tall, stately shaft before you."

5 When Edwin and his sister went back to school they meditated on their father's words; and afterwards whenever they were disposed to think lightly of small beginnings, they called to mind

the great tree in California, and so did not despair. "If," thought they, "a tree can grow so in bulk, why may not we grow in knowledge?" and they learned to be patient and hopeful.

LESSON II.

AC-CEPT', to receive; to take.
CLAIMED, demanded; required.
COW'ARD-LY, meanly timid.
FAM'I-LY, those living in the same house.
GLA'ZIER (gla'zhur), one who sets window-glass.
PACK'AGE, a bundle; a bale.
PANE, a square, particularly of glass.
READ'I-NESS, promptness.
SUN'-SHADE, a small parasol.
TEMPER, due mixture; disposition; humor; mood.

THE BROKEN PANE.

1. AT our school there was a boy of the name of Robert Rich. One day he was throwing stones, when he hit a window and broke a pane of glass. No person had seen him throw the stone. He might have slunk away and kept his act a secret, if he had not been too noble a boy to do such a meanness.

2. Mr. Hardwick, who lived in the house where the window was broken, was a lawyer, and seemed to be of a stern, harsh temper, for he used to scold the boys if they but crossed his fields, or even entered his woods. Robert did not like to meet him.

3. But Robert had more fear of doing wrong than of facing the anger of the lawyer and all his family. So he went up tc Mr. Hardwick and said, "In throwing a stone just now, I broke a pane of glass in one of your upper windows." "Well,

then, you must send a glazier and have it mended," said Mr. Hardwick in an angry tone.

4. "That is just what I wished to do," said Robert, "and I will do it at once." Struck by this manly reply, Mr. Hardwick asked Robert if he had any money to pay the glazier. "Yes," said Robert, "I have a dollar that I have been saving up."

5. "What have you been saving it up for?" asked Mr. Hardwick. "I have been saving it up to buy my sister a sun-shade," replied Robert. "Well, sir," said the lawyer, "I look to you to see that my window is mended."

6. Robert bowed and took his leave. That same day he sent a glazier and had a new pane of glass set in place of the broken one. He felt that Mr. Hardwick had claimed of him no more than was right, and he did not blame him.

7. But as Robert sat studying his lesson that evening the door-bell was rung, and a package was left for him. He opened it, and what do you think he found? In the package was a beautiful silk sun-shade, and with it a letter from Mr. Hardwick in these words: "Accept this as a proof that I was pleased by your readiness in doing right to-day."

8 Robert ran and gave the sun-shade to his sister, and she was so delighted with the gift that she almost wept in her joy. His father, when he learned what had happened, said to Robert, "We should always do right for the love of right, and not in the hope of a reward."

9. "I am sure I did not hope for a reward," said Robert. "I should still have been glad that I paid for mending the window, even if I had got nothing in return, for surely I deserved nothing. I see that a man may seem stern, like Mr. Hardwick, and yet be kind at heart."

LESSON III.

BE-GUIL'ING, cheating; deceiving.

EN-NO'BLING, making noble.

GROV'EL-ING (grŏv'vl), creeping close to the earth; mean.

IN-TEL'LI-GENCE, mental power; knowledge.

JOUR'NEYED, traveled.

MUSE, to meditate, to think.

O'ER-TAKE', a contraction of *overtake.*

QUELLED, crushed; subdued.

QUEST, the act of seeking.

SLOTH'FUL-LY, idly; lazily.

TAR'RIED, delayed; stayed.

WIST'FUL, attentive; earnest.

WORLD'LING, one devoted to worldly things.

THE STREET OF BY-AND-BY.

"By the street of 'By-and-By' one arrives at the house of 'Never.'"— *Old Saying.*

I.

OH, shun the spot, my youthful friends;
I urge you to beware!
Beguiling is the pleasant way,
And softly breathes the air;
Yet none have ever passed to scenes
Ennobling, great and high,
Who once began to linger
In the street of By-and-By.

II.

A youth aspired to climb the height
Of Learning's lofty hill:

What dimmed his bright intelligence?
What quelled his earnest will?
Why did the object of his quest
Still mock his wistful eye?
Too long, alas! he tarried
In the street of By-and-By.

III.

"My projects thrive," the merchant said;
"When doubled is my store,
How freely shall my ready gold
Be showered among the poor!"
Vast grew his wealth, yet strove he not
The mourner's tear to dry;
He never journeyed onward
From the street of By-and-By.

IV.

The wearied worldling muses
Upon lost and wasted days,
Resolved to turn hereafter
From the error of his ways—
To lift his groveling thoughts from earth,
And fix them on the sky;
Why does he linger fondly
In the street of By-and-By?

V.

Oh, shun the spot, my youthful friends;
Work on, while yet you may;
Let not old age o'ertake you
As you slothfully delay,—
Lest you should gaze around you,
And discover, with a sigh,
You have reached the house of "Never,"
Through the street of "By-and-By."

LESSON IV.

AL-LOY′, a baser metal that is mixed with a finer one.

ENGINE (ĕn′jĭn), a contrivance; a machine.

FOR′FAR-SHIRE (-sheer), a county of Scotland.

FUL-FILL′MENT, or FULFIL-MENT, completion; execution.

HERB′AGE (erb-, or herb-), pasture; grass; herbs collectively; green food for beasts.

HER′O-ISM (-izm), quality of a hero.

LAN′TERN, a case for a candle; the upper part of a lighthouse.

MUS′CU-LAR, strong; brawny.

PUL′MO-NA-RY, relating to the lungs.

REEF, a ridge of rocks near the surface of the water.

WROUGHT (rawt), worked; effected.

The *e* in *heroism* should have the sound of *e* in *terror*. Avoid introducing a decided vowel sound before the *m* in *-ism* (izm). Do not say *air* for *are* (pronounced *r*). Do not say *tremendyus* for *tre-men′dous*.

FEMALE HEROISM.

1. ON the north-eastern part of the coast of England are several small islands, known as the Fern

Islands. They are separated from the mainland by a channel not two miles broad. They are chiefly composed of rock, with here and there a slight covering of herbage.

2. On the largest of these little islands, which is called Longstone, there is a lighthouse, which in the year 1838 was kept by a man named Darling. He had a wife and several children, among whom was a daughter, Grace Darling, twenty-two years old.

3. On the night of September 6th there was a terrible storm. Grace woke up several times, and thought of the poor mariners exposed to the winds and the waves. She looked out from her little window, but could see nothing but the reflection of light from the lantern, for the sky was clouded, while the waves, wrapt in mist, were foaming furiously against the rocks.

4. Uttering a prayer for the sailors, she again lay down on her bed, but with the earliest gleam of daylight she rose and dressed herself. Then taking a spyglass, she looked out upon the rough, tumbling waters, and through the mist, to see if there were any signs of a wreck.

5. She had not looked a minute before her heart began to throb violently, for there, about a mile distant, on a reef running out into the sea, lay the remnant of a ship, while on it were human beings waiting for rescue. It was the wreck of the Forfarshire steamer.

6. This steamer had sailed the night before from

Hull on a voyage to Dundee in Scotland. At starting she had on board sixty-three persons. A storm struck her, and she leaked so badly the fires could not be kept burning, and her engines soon ceased to work. She became unmanageable, and drifted onto the reef.

7. At once all was confusion among the crew. A portion of them, including the first mate, lowered one of the boats and left the ship. With them was a single cabin passenger who threw himself into the boat by means of a rope. These men were picked up after some hours, and carried into the port of Shields.

8. A second shock, that dashed the steamer farther upon the reef, caused her to break into two pieces. The after-part, on which were most of the passengers and the captain and his wife, was swept away by a tremendous current, and all upon it were lost.

9. The fore-part of the vessel, on which were five of the crew and four passengers, stuck fast to the rock. These few survivors remained in their dreadful situation till daybreak, with a fearful sea running around them. With what anxious eyes did they wait for the morning light!

10. These were the people whom Grace saw through the spy-glass. Calling her father she pointed them out to him. What could be done? None of the family were at home except Mrs. Darling, Grace and her father. "What can we do for these poor sufferers?" asked Grace.

11. "I do not see that we can help them," replied her father. "It would be impossible for one man to manage a boat in such a sea as that. Even two men, if they attempted it, would do it at the peril of their lives." "But we must not leave those poor creatures to perish!" cried Grace. "How can we help it?" answered Mr. Darling.

12. "Father, I can pull an oar with you," exclaimed Grace. "You! Why, Grace, you never pulled an oar in such a sea as that. You haven't the strength, you haven't the courage." "Try me," said Grace;—"Oh, father, let us save them. God will give us strength, if we will but heartily venture in so good a cause."

13. Her earnest entreaties finally induced Mr. Darling to make the attempt. With the mother's assistance the boat was launched, and father and daughter entered it, each taking an oar. It was only by the exertion of great muscular strength, as well as by the utmost coolness and resolution, that they rowed the boat up to the reef amid the foam and dash of the breakers.

14. What was the amazement of the people on the wreck at seeing that one of the two coming to the rescue was a girl! As the boat drew near, it required great care to so manage it as to prevent its being dashed to pieces on the sharp ridge which had proved fatal to the steamer. With much difficulty the father scrambled up on the rock, and the boat was left for a while to the unaided skill of the daughter.

15. She proved equal to the occasion. The nine sufferers were safely rescued and conveyed to the lighthouse. The poet Wordsworth has eloquently described the scene:

> "Every hazard faced,
> And difficulty mastered, with resolve
> That no one breathing should be left to perish,
> This last remainder of the crew are all
> Placed in the little boat, then o'er the deep
> Are safely borne, landed upon the beach,
> And, in fulfillment of God's mercy, lodged
> Within the sheltering lighthouse. Shout, ye waves!
> Send forth a sound of triumph. Waves and winds,
> Exult in this deliverance, wrought through faith
> In Him whose Providence your rage has served!
> Ye screaming sea-mews, in the concert join!"

16. Grace Darling did not live long to enjoy the fame which her noble deed soon won for her. In the autumn of 1841 she showed symptoms of pulmonary disease, and though all the means of restoration which medical skill could suggest were resorted to, she gradually declined, and breathed her last in calm submission to the will of God, October 20, 1842.

17. But the memory of her act will not perish. Heroism like hers is one of the noblest attributes of the soul of man. It has no alloy of blind animal passion; it is spiritual and, we may reverently add, celestial. Never does man appear more distinctly in the image of his Maker than when, like the generous Grace Darling, he deliberately exposes his own life to save the lives of others.

LESSON V.

JAIL, a prison.
LIST′ENED (lis′snd), gave ear.
PAS′SEN-GER, one that travels.
RE-STORED′, healed; revived.
SIGNS, tokens; proofs.
SLY′LY, cunningly.

BREATHE PURE AIR.

1. SOME girls and boys were playing at hide-and-seek, when Mark Hanson saw Mary Bancroft go and hide in a large chest. Mark thought it would be good sport to lock Mary up in the chest; so he went slyly and pressed down the cover and turned the key.

2. Mary made an outcry when she found she was locked in. Mark did not heed her cries, but ran off and played for some time with the other girls and boys.

3. At last some one asked, "Where is Mary?" To which Mark replied, "I have played a good trick on Mary. Let us go now and let her out of jail." So Mark led the way to the chest, and cried, "Halloo! Do you wish to be let out?"

4. To this question no answer came. Mark listened, but could hear no noise in the trunk. He turned the key and lifted the cover. What was his horror on finding Mary motionless and senseless! An alarm was raised at once, and the doctor was sent for.

5. For more than an hour it was believed that Mary was dead. But at length she gave some signs of life. The doctor worked with new zeal, and, after much effort, she was restored. Then the

doctor turned to Mark, and said, "Were you such a little dunce as not to know that without fresh air we cannot live? Come here, girls and boys, and remember this: though we may take pure air into our lungs, we do not breathe pure air out.

6. "The air which we breathe out is not fit to be breathed in again. We soon use up, in this way, all the pure air about us. So we must have a fresh supply. As soon as Mary had breathed in all the good air that was in the trunk, there was nothing left but poisoned air. If fresh air had not been given to her by opening the trunk, she could not have lived three minutes longer.

7. "Nothing is so needful to health as good, pure air. Whether you are in the school-room or in the house, remember this. Bad air is so much poison, and the more we breathe it, the worse it gets. The poison is carbonic acid, and to breathe it long is certain death.

8. "Not many years ago, during a storm at sea, a stupid sea-captain ordered his passengers to go below in the hold of the vessel. Then he covered up the hold, so that no fresh air could enter. When the storm was over he opened the hold, and found that seventy human beings had died for want of pure air.

9. "Through his gross ignorance of the laws of life he had done all this mischief. Remember, boys, what I say: insist on having good air; for impure air, though it may not always kill you, is always bad for your health."

LESSON VI.

AL-LOT'TED, granted; given.
AP-PEAR'ANCE, coming in sight.
AP-POINT'ED, fixed upon.
AR-RANGED', put in place.
AR'TI-CLES, distinct things.
DE-POS'IT-ING, placing.
IN-CLOSED' or EN-CLOSED', shut in; fenced; encompassed.
GROUPS (groops), small crowds.
LIN'EN, cloth of flax or hemp.
MA-NURE', anything that fertilizes land.
PRONE, habitually inclined.
REF'USE, worthless remains.
RUB'BISH, things waste or cast away.
SCAV'EN-GER (skav'en-jer), one who cleans streets.
SEP'A-RAT-ING, dividing from the rest.
WAG'ON, a vehicle on four wheels.
WOOL'EN or WOOL'LEN, made of wool.
YON'DER, at a distance within view.

Give *u* in *manure, fortune, manufacturer*, its *y* sound as in *mute*. Do not say *manoor, fortoon*, etc. Do not say *narrer* for *nar'row, wheelbarrer* for *wheel-bar'row, fust* for *first, appinted* for *ap-point'ed*.

EVERY THING IS OF USE.

1. YOUNG people are too prone to waste. Listen to a true story. When I was a young man I lived in London, and lodged in a very narrow street. There came to this street, once or twice a week, a man of the name of Bryant. He would come with a wheelbarrow and a broom, sweep the street, and carry off all the refuse.

2. In the course of a few months, Bryant made his appearance with a small cart, drawn by a donkey, and not long after, he came with a wagon and horses. The next year he had quite a number of wagons and horses, and became the scavenger of a large part of London. And what do you think he did with the masses of filth which he collected?

3. He hired a large field not far from the city;

he inclosed it with a wall, in which there were twelve or fifteen gates, and at each of these gates you might see wagons entering and depositing their contents in heaps. On these heaps might be seen groups of women and children, hired for the purpose, poking and scraping, with a view of separating articles of the same class or kind, and laying these in places by themselves.

4. Here is a piece of black iron—that goes there. Here is a bit of white iron, or tin—that goes yonder. Here is a rag of linen, or one of cotton cloth—these are placed on the spot allotted to each. Here is an old hat—that goes to its appointed corner. And so with bits of leather, and of rope, with scraps of woolen stuff, with bones, the horns and hoofs of oxen and sheep, and with each of a great mass of other things.

5. Now, having thus collected and arranged all this rubbish and refuse, Bryant found a use, and a profitable use, too, for every one of the various articles which had been thrown away as utterly useless. His linen rags he sold to the paper-makers; his bits of brass and iron, to brass and iron founders; his pieces of bone and horns, either to farmers for manure, or to the manufacturers of knife-handles and combs.

6. Gradually and laboriously he extended his trade, and at last retired with a large fortune. Many years after the time when I first saw him with his wheelbarrow, I found him, an elderly man, riding about the streets in his carriage. From

his experience you may see that everything is of use, and may be turned to account. There is nothing that should be reckoned utterly worthless, and a thousand things might be turned to some good purpose that are every hour heedlessly thrown away.

LESSON VII.

DE-RI'SION (de-rizh'un), mockery; contempt by laughter.

DOZ'EN (duz'zn), twelve.

FAITH'FUL, firm to the truth.

FEAT, an act; an exploit.

RE-PLIED', answered.

SHRUG, a drawing up of the shoulders. (Do not say *srug* for *shrug*.)

TRAV'EL-ER or TRAV'EL-LER, one who travels.

WE'LL, a contraction of *we will.*

WIT'NESS-ES, persons who see and testify.

YARD, a measure of three feet.

YON, a short distance off.

YOU'LL, a contraction of *you will.*

THE BOASTING TRAVELER.

I.

A FELLOW who had been in Rome
Was boasting to the folks at home.

II.

"Once, when I was in Rome," he said,
"A leap of twenty yards I made
Over a bar placed ten feet high:
A dozen witnesses were by."

III.

His hearers at each other wink,
Or by a shrug tell what they think.

IV.

"Come on," says one who near him stood;
"Yon empty ditch and fence of wood

Are not by half so high or wide;
Here let the feat again be tried."

V.

"Yes," cried another, "if you'll do
But half, we'll think your story true.
Suppose yourself at Rome, and we
Your faithful witnesses will be."

VI.

The man replied: "Ah! I to-day
Am not quite well," then stole away,
While bursts of laughter, long and loud,
Told the derision of the crowd.

VII.

Avoid the boasting vein, if you
Would not be scorned and laughed at too.

LESSON VIII.

DOCK'-YARD, a place where ships are built or repaired.
DON'T, a contraction of *do not.*
HULL, the body of a ship.
IM-MENSE', very great.
IN'FLU-ENCE, a directing power.
LAUNCHED (länched), moved into the water.
MASS'IVE, heavy; bulky.
OFT'EN (of'n), frequently.
SUG-GEST'(sug-jest' or sud-jest'), to hint.

WHAT A LITTLE HELP MAY DO.

1. WE have somewhere read that at an English dockyard a great ship was to be launched: an immense multitude assembled to see it glide down the slides that were to send it into the water. The blocks and wedges were knocked away, but the massive hull did not stir, and there was disappointment.

2. Just then a little boy ran forward, and began to push the ship with all his might. The crowd broke out into a laugh of ridicule, but it so happened that the vessel was almost ready to move: the few pounds pushed by the lad were all that were needed to start it, and away it went into the water.

3. This teaches an important lesson to every boy and girl. You often think that the little you can do is of no account. You don't know that. A little word, a kind act, however small, may be, and often is, the turning-point in one's own history, and sometimes of great importance in its influence upon others.

4. A good deed, or the resistance of a temptation, may start up good thoughts in the mind of a playmate and lead to other good thoughts and deeds. The train of thought in one's mind is like a train of cars. The little iron frog or tongue on the rail, no larger than your finger at its point, may direct the locomotive upon the right track, or, if wrongly placed, may turn the engine aside, and hurl it down a steep bank to fearful destruction. So the smallest word may start the mind on a right or wrong track.

5. Young friends, your little words, little thoughts and little works are important. Strive earnestly to be right, noble, generous, at all times, in secret and in public. When, in the future, we come to see the great map of human action spread out, it will be found that we have been daily exert-

ing an influence that is affecting the characters of all with whom we come in contact. Give a good push at the ship: do a good deed, no matter how trifling, whenever and wherever you can, and trust to God for the result.

LESSON IX.

CAN'T, a contraction of *can not.*

COUNT'ER, the table of a shop on which money is counted.

CRICK'ET, an insect; a stool; a game.

DON'T, a contraction of *do not.*

HEARTH (härth), a place for a fire under a chimney.

HUR'RIED, did hurry.

MA'AM, a contraction of *madam.*

ROGUE (rōg), a knave.

SOUGHT, did seek.

THE BOY WHO WANTED A CRICKET.

1. ONCE, on the first of April, a little boy went out into the streets of a large city to see if he could find such a thing as a live cricket. He looked by

the side of all the trees, and in every place where a blade of grass was to be seen, but nowhere could he find what he sought.

2. At last he stopped a man and said, "Please, sir, have you such a thing as a cricket you could give me?" The man took him by the ear and replied, "You little rogue! you think to make an April fool of me, do you? What is your name, sir?"

3. My name is Frank May," said the little boy, "and I'll thank you to let go of my ear." "Well, Frank, you must not play tricks on travelers," said the man as he pinched the lad's ear and walked on. Then Frank saw a boy of his own age, and went up to him and asked, "Do your folks have such a thing as a live cricket in the house?"

4. "That means you want to have a fight, does it?" replied the boy. "Well, I'm ready for you. You will be the third fellow I have fought to-day." And the boy threw down his hat, took off his jacket, and rolled up the sleeves of his shirt.

5. Frank said that he had not come out for a fight; that he had no time for a fight; that he had come out for a cricket, and a cricket he must find. "But if you can't get along without a fight," added Frank, "come on quick, because I'm in a hurry."

6. "Oh, go and find your cricket," said the boy. So Frank walked on till he came to a baker's shop, where he saw three women behind a counter, and loaves of bread on the shelves.

Frank went into the shop, and said to one of the women, "Please, ma'am, can you let me have a cricket?" "We sell bread here, not crickets, my little man," said the woman. "But what do you want with a cricket?"

7. "Don't crickets on the hearth bring good luck?" asked Frank. "Well, I have heard folks say so," replied the woman, "but I think they said it in jest. The best way to get good luck is to seize it by hard work. That is the way I got all *my* good luck."

8. "My mother has worked till she is ill," said Frank, "and last night I woke up late and found her crying, and now I want her to have some good luck." "Have you no father?" asked the shop-woman. "My father was lost at sea last spring," said Frank. "And how many children has your mother?" "She has three in all, and I am the oldest." "And how old are you, little boy?" "I shall be seven years old next June."

9. "Well, my boy," said the woman, "now take these three loaves of bread home to your mother, and then come back and see me." With a glad smile Frank said, "Thank you!" and took the bread. He hurried home with it, and then hurried back to see the good woman.

10. She said, "I know you must be a good boy, for you love your mother. I cannot give you a cricket, but I can give you a place as an errand-boy in our shop. Only do well, and your mother's luck lies with you, and not with the crickets."

11. Frank *did* do well—so well that he never woke up after that in the night to find his dear mother shedding tears. By his good conduct he helped and cheered her so that she had no cause to weep, unless it was with joy.

LESSON X.

PAT′RON-AGE, support; protection.
ATE (āte or ĕt), preterit of *eat*.
AP-PRO-BA′TION, act of approving; a liking.
RES′O-LUTE, bold; firm.

THE EXCELLENT MAN.

I.

THEY gave me advice and plenty of praise,
Promised to help me in various ways,
Said that I only should "wait a while,"
And offered their patronage with a smile.

II.

But with all their honor and approbation,
I should long ago have died of starvation,
If an excellent man, with a resolute heart,
Had not come forward to take my part.

III.

Good fellow! he got me the food I ate;
His kindness and care I can never forget;
Yet I cannot embrace him, though other folks can,
For I myself am that excellent man.

BE GRATEFUL.

SMALL service is true service while it lasts;
Of friends, however humble, scorn not one;
The daisy, by the shadow that it casts,
Protects the lingering dew-drop from the sun.

LESSON XI.

AN-TIP′O-DES, those people who, living on the opposite side of the globe, have their feet directly opposite to ours.

PRE-POS′TER-OUS, inverted in order; absurd.

PRE-SEN′TI-MENT, a foreboding a previous notion or idea.

THE RETURN OF COLUMBUS.

Don Gomez. What is this wild story you have heard, sir? Columbus returned? The east discovered by sailing westwardly? Impossible!

Secretary. It is even so, Don Gomez. A courier has just arrived at the palace with the news. Columbus was driven by stress of weather to anchor in the Tagus. All Portugal is in a ferment of enthusiasm, and all Spain will be equally excited soon. The sensation is prodigious.

Don G. But did I not denounce this man's scheme at the outset? Did I not warn her Majesty against him? And now you tell me he has found a new world. Oh, it is all a trick!

Sec. But he has brought home the proofs of his visit: gold and precious stones; strange plants and animals; parrots like those from remote parts of Asia; and above all, specimens of a new race of men, copper-colored, with straight hair.

Don G. Still, I say, a trick! He has been coasting along the African shore, and has there collected a few curiosities which he is passing off for proofs of his pretended discovery.

Sec. It is a little singular that all his men should be leagued with him in keeping up so unprofitable a falsehood.

Don G. But 'tis against reason, against common sense, that such a discovery should be made. As one of her Majesty's council, I proved conclusively long ago that Columbus was a mere pretender. Why, sir, he argued that the earth is a globe and capable of being circumnavigated!

Sec. King John of Portugal has received him with great favor, has listened to his accounts, and is persuaded that they are true.

Don G. King John is— Well, sir, he is not a plain, matter-of-fact man like myself. I am not to be taken in by any such preposterous story. This vaunted discovery will turn out to be no discovery at all. With my compass and my map, did I not prove that it was impossible? But the queen would not be convinced.

Sec. The king and queen have ordered grand preparations for the reception of Columbus.

Don G. What delusion! Her Majesty is so credulous! It is hard to make her listen to a plain, matter-of-fact man like me. Why, sir, she told me the other day that I was an old bore. Think of that, sir! I a bore!

Sec. Is it possible, Don Gomez, that she made such a remark? But then you must remember she is a woman. She says she pledged her jewels to fit Columbus out on his voyage, and that she has had a presentiment from the first that he would succeed.

Don G. A presentiment! How like a woman! Instead of a reason she gives us a presentiment.

I am a matter-of-fact *man*, sir; and mark my words: it will all turn out a trick—mere moonshine. The crews of the vessels may have been deceived; Columbus may have steered a southerly course instead of a westerly. Anything is probable rather than that a continent to the west of us has been discovered.

Sec. I saw the courier who brought the news. He told me he had conversed with all the sailors, and they laughed at the notion that there could be any mistake about the discovery, or that any other than a westerly course had been steered.

Don G. Still, I say, a trick! What, sir! am I to believe that the earth is a globe, and that men are standing with their heads down in space, with the soles of their feet opposite to ours?

Sec. It *is* rather hard, I admit, to believe that. If it were so, what would prevent the water from flowing out of all the wells? Every step I take on the flat earth disproves that notion.

Don G. To be sure! What, sir! An ignorant sailor from Genoa in the right, and all our men of learning, not to speak of her Majesty's chief councilor, in the wrong! Nonsense! I'm a matter-of-fact man, sir, and I hate all innovators. I will believe what I can see and handle and comprehend, but as for believing in the antipodes, or that Columbus has found a continent to the west of us— Ring the bell, sir; call my carriage; I will go to the palace and undeceive the king. The dignity of Spain must be saved. I must save it.

LESSON XII.

BAN, to curse; to interdict.

FORGE (fōrj), a furnace in which metals are heated for hammering into form.

PER′IL, danger; hazard.

PU′NY, petty; inferior.

SHIRK, to get off from; to slink away.

SUC′COR, help; relief.

WRITH′ING, twisting; distorting.

THE GIANT AND THE DWARF.

I.

As on through life's journey we go day by day,
There are two whom we meet at each turn of the way,
To help or to hinder, to bless or to ban,
And the names of these two are "I Can't" and "I Can."

II.

"I Can't" is a dwarf, a poor, pale, puny imp,
His eyes are half blind, and his walk is a limp.
He stumbles and falls, or lies writhing with fear,
Though dangers are distant and succor is near.

III.

"I Can" is a giant: unbending he stands;
There is strength in his arms and skill in his hands;
He asks for no favors, he wants but a share
Where labor is honest and wages are fair.

IV.

"I Can't" is a sluggard, too lazy to work,
From duty he shrinks, every task he will shirk;
No bread on his board, no meal in his bag,
His house is a ruin, his coat is a rag.

V.

"I Can" is a worker; he tills the broad fields,
And digs from the earth all the wealth which it yields;
The hum of his spindle begins with the light,
And the fires of his forges are blazing all night.

VI.

"I Can't" is a coward half fainting with fright;
At the first thought of peril he slinks out of sight;
Skulks and hides till the noise of the battle is past,
Or sells his best friends, and turns traitor at last.

VII.

"I Can" is a hero, the first in the field,
Though others may falter, he never will yield;
He makes the long marches, he deals the last blow
His charge is the whirlwind that scatters the foe.

VIII.

How grandly and nobly he stands to his trust,
When, roused at the call of a cause that is just,
He weds his strong will to the valor of youth,
And writes on his banner the watchword of truth!

IX.

Then up and be doing! the day is not long;
Throw fear to the winds, be patient and strong!
Stand fast in your place, act your part like a man,
And when duty calls, answer promptly, "I can!"

VIRTUE AND ERROR.

MANY there are who of their lot complain;
Many there are who rail at fate in vain;
But on himself weak man should vent his rage:
Error in youth must lead to gloom in age.

Many there are content in humblest lot;
Many there are, though poor, who murmur not;
Write, then, in gold, on their recording page,
Virtue in youth must lead to bliss in age.

LESSON XIII.

DIC'TATE, to tell what to write; to order.
DIS-AS'TER, calamity; mishap.
HEEL, to lean on one side.
LIEU-TEN'ANT (lu-ten'ant, or lef-ten'ant), an officer next below a captain in rank.
LIGHT'ER, a large boat used in loading or unloading ships.
NEC'ES-SA-RY (nes'-), indispensable
PORT-HOLE, a hole to point cannon through.
RES'CUE, a deliverance.
SHEATH, a case; a scabbard.
SHROUDS (heed the sound of *sh*), large ropes which help to support the masts of a ship.
VIS'IT-OR, one who visits.

THE LOSS OF THE "ROYAL GEORGE."

1. IN the month of August, 1782, a sad calamity took place at Spithead by which many hundreds of brave sailors suddenly found a watery grave. They belonged to the "Royal George," a fine ship which carried one hundred guns. She was the finest ship of the English fleet, and Admiral Kempenfelt's blue flag floated from one of her masts.

2. When nearly ready to go to sea, it was found by the first lieutenant that the water-pipe was out of order. It was not thought necessary to put the vessel into dock in order to repair her, but only to "heel" her over—that is, weigh her down on one side till the damaged part was above water and the workmen could do what was required.

3. A number of men were sent from one of the dockyards to help the carpenters in their work. The great guns on one side were run out as far as possible, and those on the other side were brought into the middle of the ship. This made her lean

over as much as was needful, and so the workmen got at the mouth of the water-pipe which wanted mending.

4. Just then a lighter came alongside the "Royal George" laden with casks of rum; and a large number of men were told to take them on board. The port-holes were almost level with the water before the arrival of the lighter, and, when the men went to take in the casks, the ship "heeled" over still more, and the water began to wash into the lower-deck ports.

5. The carpenter saw the peril that both ship and crew were in, and ran to the second lieutenant, who was on duty, and told him of it. The lieutenant was angry that the carpenter should "presume to dictate to him," and ordered him back to his work. A breeze began to rise, and, seeing the danger increase, the man went a second time to the officer, and warned him that all would be lost if the ship was not righted instantly, but he only received oaths for his pains.

6. The lieutenant, however, at length ordered the drummer to summon the men, in order to put the guns in their usual places, but it was too late. Before the drum could be beaten the water was rushing in fast at the open port-holes, and, almost before help or rescue could be as much as thought of, the brave ship sank, carrying down with her the admiral, officers, men, and visitors on board to the number of many hundred souls.

7. So sudden was the disaster that only a few

who happened to be on the upper deck could save themselves. Admiral Kempenfelt was in his cabin writing when he and all his crew thus perished on a fair day, in sight of land, and surrounded by a fleet of ships. This remarkable event has been described by Cowper in the following little poem:

I.

Toll for the brave—the brave that are no more!
All sunk beneath the wave, fast by their native shore!
Eight hundred of the brave, whose courage well was tried,
Had made the vessel heel, and laid her on her side.
A land-breeze shook the shrouds, and she was overset;
Down went the Royal George with all her crew complete!

II.

Toll for the brave! Brave Kempenfelt is gone;
His last sea-fight is fought—his work of glory done.
It was not in the battle; no tempest gave the shock;
She sprang no fatal leak; she ran upon no rock.
His sword was in its sheath, his fingers held the pen,
When Kempenfelt went down with twice four hundred men.

III.

Weigh the vessel up once dreaded by our foes,
And mingle with our cup the tear that England owes.
Her timbers yet are sound, and she may float again,
Full charged with England's thunder, and plow the distant main.
But Kempenfelt is gone; his victories are o'er,
And he and his eight hundred shall plow the wave no more.

QUESTIONS, ETC.—Describe the accident to the Royal George. What was the date of the disaster? Who was most to blame for it? What English poet wrote some verses in commemoration of the event? Who was Cowper? (An eminent English poet, born 1731, died 1800.)

LESSON XIV.

A-POL′O-GY, an expression of regret for an offense; an excuse.
CAS′TLE (käs′sl), a fortified house.
CON-SID′ER-ATE, thoughtful.
EARL (erl), a title of English nobility.
EN-SUED′, followed.
GOV′ERN-ESS, a female tutor.
IM PRES′SION, a mark made by pressure; influence; effect.
IN′TER-VIEW, a formal meeting.
PAS′SEN-GER, one that travels.
PRE-TENSE′ or PRE′TENCE, a false show or reason.
RE′AL-LY, in truth; truly.
SCEN′ER-Y, objects of a scene.

THE OUTSIDE PASSENGER.

1. SOME years ago, in England, on a fine day in August, a young lady took a seat in a stage-coach. For many miles she rode alone; but there was enough to amuse her in the scenery through which she passed, and in the pleasing hopes that filled her mind.

2. She had been engaged as governess for the grandchildren of an earl, and was now on her way to his castle. At midday the coach stopped at an inn, and she alighted, and sat down at the table. An elderly man followed, and sat down also.

3. The young lady arose, rang the bell, and addressing the waiter, said, "Here is an outside passenger; I can not dine with an outside passenger." The stranger bowed, saying, "I beg your pardon, madam; I can go into another room," and immediately retired. The coach soon afterward resumed its course, and the passengers their places.

4. At length the coach stopped at the gate leading to the castle to which the young lady was going; but there was not such prompt attention as she expected, for all eyes seemed directed to the outside passenger, who was preparing to dismount. The young lady beckoned, and was answered, "As soon as we have attended to his lordship, we will come to you."

5. A few words of explanation ensued. To her dismay, the young lady found that the outside passenger, with whom she had thought it beneath her to dine, was not only a nobleman, but that very nobleman in whose family she hoped to be an inmate. What could she do? How could she bear the interview? She felt really ill when she thought of her rudeness; and the apology she sent that evening for not appearing in the presence of the family was sincere.

6. The venerable peer was a kind and consid-

erate man. He sent for the foolish girl, and reasoned with her on her conduct at the inn. He insisted on the impropriety of the state of mind which it showed, and told her that nothing could induce him to allow his children to be taught such notions.

7. He refused to accept any apology that did not go to the length of acknowledging that her conduct was wrong; and, when the right impression seemed to be produced, he gave her his hand in friendship.

OVER THE FENCE.

BOY.

OVER the fence is a garden fair—
How I would love to be master there!
All that I lack is a mere pretense—
Then I could leap that low white fence.

CONSCIENCE.

This is the way all crimes commence:
Sin and sorrow are over the fence.

BOY.

Over the fence I can toss my ball,
Then I can go for it—that is all;
Picking an apple beneath a tree
Would not be really theft, you see.

CONSCIENCE.

That is a falsehood—a weak pretense;
Sin and sorrow are over the fence.

BOY.

Whose is the whisper so low and plain?
Twice have I heard it, and not in vain;
I will not venture a look that way,—
From honor and right I will not stray.

CONSCIENCE.

Remember, remember, all crimes commence
With coveting that which is over the fence.

LESSON XV.

AN'SWERED (an'serd), replied to.
AT-TAIN', to come to; to gain.
BUILD'ING, a fabric; an edifice.
CON'SCIENCE, the faculty of knowing right from wrong.
ES-SEN'TIAL (-shal), necessary.
EX-AM'INE (egz-am'in), to search into.
FI-DEL'I-TY, adherence to truth.
MA-CHIN'ER-Y (ma-sheen'er-y), the works of a machine.
MO-NI'TIONS (-nish'uns), warnings.
PA'TIENT (pa'shent), enduring.
PRUS'SIAN (prŭsh'an), belonging to Prussia.
ROTE, mere repetition.
SPIN'DLE, a pin to form thread on.
SU-PE-RI-OR'I-TY, the state of being superior.
VAL'U-A-BLE, having worth.
WEAV'ER, one who weaves.

IMPORTANCE OF THOUGHT.

1. I ONCE asked a number of children the common question, Which is the heavier, a pound of feathers or a pound of lead? Some answered at once, "A pound of lead, to be sure," but others *thought*, and then said, "They are both alike; a pound is a pound."

2. I have known some children, who, when learning the multiplication table, were not satisfied with learning it merely by rote, but would examine

and count out each sum till they had found out for themselves that it was all true. These children had the reward of patient thought.

3. All have heard the saying, "There is no royal road to learning." This means, simply, that no one can think for another; each one must think patiently for himself. We would like much to see things at a glance without any trouble. Some see quicker than others, but all who would attain to any real superiority must think patiently for themselves.

4. Have you ever been in a cotton factory? If so, you saw there hundreds of spindles, whirling and spinning the cotton fine and even, and faster than you could think. You saw the looms of the weavers, each with its swift shuttle flying backward and forward, just as if it knew of itself what it was about, and the weaver had only to watch and wait upon it; and, perhaps, you saw the huge wheel turning round and round so gracefully, so majestically, and keeping everything moving in the whole building like a great living heart of the whole.

5. What has done all this? What has invented and contrived all this wonderful machinery? The patient thought of a few minds. It was not at the first glance that they saw all these miracles which they have produced, but they thought it all out patiently and laboriously, till they found the way to do these things.

6. What was it but patient thought that taught

Columbus that there must be a western continent? What but patient thought taught Fulton how he might give to mankind the steamboat? It was patient thought that enabled Washington to conduct the great affairs of war and peace, with which he was intrusted, to a successful issue. It was by patient thought that Napoleon saw how he might conquer his enemies in the field and place France at the head of the nations; and it was by patient thought that the great Prussian general planned the conquest of France.

7. Nothing truly great or valuable has been, or ever will be, accomplished without patient thought. By thought alone can we make ourselves wiser and better, for we are made thinking beings, and the more we occupy the mind with good thoughts, the truer, the nobler and the happier we are.

8. Patient thought is essential to the study of the will and purposes of the Creator, and of our duties and relations to him and to each other. Thought tells us that the monitions of a pure conscience are the accents of his voice ever speaking to us, and that there is no true peace for us except in fidelity to our sense of right and in obedience to the will of God.

9. I once knew a little girl who, after a quarrel in which she had said some unkind thing to her sister, went and sat down on the step of the door to enjoy the beautiful moonlight evening. She looked up a long while at the silent stars and at the quiet, gentle moon, and the longer and further

she looked into the depths of the heavens, the more she thought of the love and the power of Him who made all things.

10. At last she said to herself, "He who made this glorious and beautiful world must wish all to be good, all to be happy, and I have been destroying the peace and harmony of his world; but for *me* all would be good and beautiful!" She ran in to her sister, and took her by the hand, and said, "I am sorry for my unkindness to you; forgive me, and come and enjoy with me the beautiful moon and stars that God has made for us all to enjoy."

11. Thus will thought, patient thought, teach us that love is not only right, but more happy than hatred, truth more noble, more desirable than falsehood, and that no suffering which right-doing can bring upon us is equal to the torment of a bad conscience.

LESSON XVI.

Ant (ănt), a well-known insect.	**Jour′neyed**, traveled.
Boun′te-ous, free in giving.	**Lan′tern**, a case for a light.
Con-veyed′, transmitted; bore.	**Lus′ter** or **Lus′tre**, brightness.

THE ANT AND THE GLOW-WORM.

A FABLE.

I.

When night had spread its darkest shade,
And even the stars no light conveyed,
A little ant of humble gait
Was plodding homeward somewhat late.

II.

Rejoiced was she to keep in sight
A splendid glow-worm's useful light,
Which, like a lantern clear, bestowed
Its help along her dangerous road.

III.

On as she went with footstep firm,
She thus addressed the glittering worm:
"A blessing, neighbor, on your light!
I thank you for it. So, good-night!"

IV.

"What!" said the vain though gifted thing;
"Do *you* employ the light I bring?
If so, I'll keep it out of view;
I do not shine for such as you."
Its light it proudly then withdrew.

V.

A traveler, as he journeyed by,
Had seen with pleased and curious eye
The beauteous luster, now put out;
But, left in darkness and in doubt,
Unconsciously he stepped aside,
And crushed the glow-worm in its pride.

VI.

God, in his wise and bounteous love,
Has given us talents to improve;
And those who hide the precious store
May do much harm, but suffer more.

QUESTIONS, ETC.—Tell in your own words the fable of the ant and the glow-worm. What is the moral? If you do not impart all the light you have, who may suffer besides those you would deprive? What do you understand by a *fable?* (A fictitious story with a moral.)

LESSON XVII.

BAL'CO-NY, a platform on the outside of a house.
COUN'SEL, to advise.
CRAFT'Y, cunning; artful.
CREV'ICE, a cleft; a rent.
CUR'TAIN (-tĭn), a cloth hanging at a window, etc.
DE-TACHED', separated.
EAVES, the edges of the roof of a house.
FA-MIL'IAR, easy; intimate.
IN-GE-NU'I-TY, invention; skill.
JOIN'ER, one who does the woodwork in finishing buildings, etc.
MA'SON, a builder in stone or brick.
OB'STI-NATE, stubborn; perverse.
PRE-CAU'TION, previous care.
REC'OM-PENSED, rewarded.
SEN'TI-NEL, a soldier on guard.
UN-TI'DY, not neat.

THE HOUSE SPARROW.

1. No sooner is the common house sparrow occupied in making his nest than a new sentiment manifests itself in him—the love of offspring. He must think of providing a shelter for his little ones. This occupation at first makes him a little serious, but no sooner has he picked up the first blade of straw than he is filled with joy.

The bird detaching a piece of the mortar

2. He returns a hundred times a day, carrying building material in his beak; he chirps as if he

were pleased with himself, flies back again, returns to the meadows, goes, comes, and so on, all day long, looking, without appearing to do so, to see if any one is at the window, or if there are enemies behind the curtain. The sparrow is better able to see you than you are to conceal yourself.

3. He is an impudent, familiar and obstinate little bird. A sparrow was once so untidy as to soil my sleeve with a piece of mortar he had detached from the eaves of my house. I immediately sent for a joiner, telling him to cover every hole with boards, and employ all his ingenuity to prevent the smallest sparrow from penetrating any of the crevices to build his nest. The joiner worked all day to do this; but, three days after, the birds, by exploring the roof, by examining and watching, and by striking the planks with their beaks, had defeated the skill and precaution of the joiner.

4. Then I sent for a mason, and begged him to stop up the smallest holes with plaster. I afterward watched attentively myself, determined not to be played with again by these rogues of sparrows. I was soon convinced that it was impossible to baffle their skill when they are resolved on nest-building.

5. Two sparrows, more clear-sighted than the rest, in spite of all the precautions I had taken, and notwithstanding my constant presence at the window, were able to find a place for nests. They succeeded so well in penetrating the boards that

my own contrivance had enabled them to construct a snug dwelling, well sheltered from the weather, and far out of my reach.

6. I was, however, recompensed for my forbearance by being witness of a very touching scene. When the little ones were able to come out of the nest, one of them, being perched up so high, tumbled on to the balcony and hurt itself so that it could not fly.

7. Then all the sparrows from the neighboring trees and hedges, from the oldest to the youngest, came on the balcony, bringing to the poor little fellow, in their bills, the tenderest consolation. The young ones came while I was present; the old ones, more experienced and crafty, knew perfectly at what time in the day I was absent, and did not fail to come and counsel the poor disabled bird.

8. This lasted three days and nights, during which my sparrow retired to a chair in the corner of the balcony, and slept peaceably, having at his side two other large jolly fellows, to serve as sentinels. On the fourth day the little wounded one departed, joyous as a boy returning from school.

A WINTER EVENING AT HOME.

Now stir the fire and close the shutters fast,
Let fall the curtain, wheel the sofa round;
And while the bubbling and loud-hissing urn
Sends up a steamy column, and the cups
Which cheer, but not inebriate, wait on each,
So let us welcome cheerful evening in.—COWPER.

LESSON XVIII.

QUAR'RY, the object of the chase; the game of a bird of prey; a pit where stones are cut from the earth.

HYMN OF THE MOUNTAINEERS.

First Voice.

FOR the strength of the hills we bless thee, our God, our fathers' God!
Thou hast made thy children mighty by the touch of the mountain sod.
Thou hast fixed our ark of refuge where the spoiler's foot ne'er trod;—

All.

For the strength of the hills we bless thee, our God, our fathers' God!

Second Voice.

We are watchers of a beacon whose light must never die;
We are guardians of an altar mid the silence of the sky;
The rocks yield founts of courage, struck forth as by thy rod;—

All.

For the strength of the hills we bless thee, our God, our fathers' God!

Third Voice.

For the dark resounding caverns, where thy still, small voice is heard;
For the strong pines of the forest that by thy breath are stirred;
For the storms on whose free pinions thy spirit walks abroad;—

All.

For the strength of the hills we bless thee, our God, our fathers' God!

Fourth Voice.

The royal eagle darteth on his quarry from the heights,
And the stag that knows no master seeks there his wild
delights;
But we, for *thy* communion, have sought the mountain sod;—

All.

For the strength of the hills we bless thee, our God, our
fathers' God!

Fifth Voice.

The banner of the chieftain far, far below us waves;
The war-horse of the spearman cannot reach our lofty caves;
Thy dark clouds wrap the threshold of Freedom's last abode;—

All.

For the strength of the hills we bless thee, our God, our
fathers' God!

Sixth Voice.

For the shadow of thy presence, round our camp of rock
outspread;
For the stern defiles of battle, bearing record of our dead;
For the snows and for the torrents, for the free heart's burial
sod;—

All.

For the strength of the hills, we bless thee, our God, our
fathers' God!

LESSON XIX.

FRAY, a battle; a fight; a riot.
HOST, any great multitude.
SLAUGH'TER, butchery; carnage.
TRO'PHY, something taken in battle.
WAR'RIOR (war'yur), a soldier.

THE BRAVE.

WHO are the brave? the warriors bold
That slaughter their fellow-man for gold?
That risk their lives in the battle fray?
Daring they are—not brave alway!

The truly brave are the suffering host
That never of wealth had chance to boast,
Yet never have fallen or turned aside
From the path of truth, or of honest pride,—
But who spurn the tempter, come what may,
That their lives may be pure as the open day;
Who ask not a trophy to deck their grave:
The honest and poor are the truly brave!

LESSON XX.

E-LIC'IT (e-lis'it), to draw out.

EX-CLU'SIVE-LY, without admitting another.

HOV'ER-ING (hŏv'-), hanging over.

I-DE'A, thought; notion.

IN'DI-CATE, to point out; to show.

O-PAQUE' (o-pake'), not transparent.

PROB'LEM, a question for solution.

SUG-GES'TION, hint; intimation.

OBJECT TEACHING.

1. THE children having clapped hands and sung together, sang their way out of the great room in file, while others began streaming in. We were invited to an object lesson, and marched off to a class-room, where we took our seats among the pupils, whose age varied between eight years and eleven. The teacher was before us. We were all attention. "Hands down." We did it. "Hands on knees." Very good. The lesson began.

2. "I have something in my pocket," said our teacher, "which I am always glad to have there." We were old enough and worldly enough to know what he meant, but boys aspire to fill their pockets with so many things that, according to their minds,

the something in the teacher's pocket might be string, apple, knife, brass button, top, candy, wood for boat, crumbs, squirt, gunpowder, marbles, slate pencil, pea-shooter, brad-awl, or perhaps small cannon.

3. They attempted no rash guess, therefore, at that stage of the problem. "Boys also," our teacher continued, "like to have it, though when it gets into a boy's pocket, I believe that it is often said to burn a hole there." Instantly twenty outstretched hands indicated an idea demanding utterance in twenty heads. "If you please, sir, I know what it is." "What is it?" "A piece of coal."

4. "You draw your reasoning, my boy, from a part only of the information given to you, founding your view of things on the last words that sounded in your ears. We laughed at you cheerfully, but when we see the same thing done in the world daily by your elders, we do not always find it a laughing matter.

5. "This little thing in my pocket," the teacher continued, "has not much power by itself, but when many of the same kind come together they can do great deeds. A number of them have assembled lately to build handsome monuments to a great man whose name you all ought to know, for he made the penny loaf bigger than it used to be. Do you know what great man that was?"

6. Hands were out, answers were ready, but they ran pretty exclusively in favor of Prince Albert

and the Duke of Wellington.* "I am sure," says the teacher, "you must have heard who made all the loaves larger without altering the price. Think again: who was it?" A confident voice hazarded the suggestion that it was "Guy Fawkes," and half a dozen voices cried, "Guy Fawkes!" There are always some to follow the absurdest lead, if it be taken confidently, in the great as in the little world.

7. "Guy Fawkes! nonsense! Is he to be carried about in your heads all through November and December?" More inquiry at length elicited, after a little uncertain hovering about Louis Napoleon, the decisive opinion that the man who made bread cheaper was Sir Robert Peel. "If you please, sir," said an argumentative little fellow, "*he* did not make the penny loaf bigger."

8. "Why not?" "He did not make the loaf: he made the baker make it." The difficulty thus started having been properly gone into, and further statement of the riddle having been given, it was at length fairly guessed that the teacher's object upon which he meant to talk with us that day was a penny.

---

* Prince Albert, the consort or husband of Queen Victoria of England, died 1861. The Duke of Wellington, one of England's greatest generals, died 1852. Guy Fawkes, one of the originators of a plot for blowing up the House of Lords in London with gunpowder, was executed in the year 1606. Sir Robert Peel, a great English statesman, died by a fall from his horse in 1850. Charles Dickens, the author of this amusing sketch of "Object Teaching," was born in Portsmouth, England, 1812, and died 1870. As a novelist and humorist he ranks among the foremost in English literature.

9. We ascertained that it was round, that it was hard, that it was brown, that it was heavy—by which we meant, as some of us explained, that it was heavier than the same quantity of water—that it was stamped on both sides, and so forth; also that it was made of copper. Pence being next regarded purely in the light of copper, the name of the metal, "copper," was written at the top of a blackboard, and a line was drawn, along which we were to place a regiment of qualities.

10. We began easily by asserting copper to be hard, and showed our penetration by discovering that, since a penny would not do for framing as a spy-glass, it must be opaque. Can you spell *opaque?* Oh dear, yes! Twenty hands were out, but we were not all so wise as we imagined. No matter; there are folks of larger size elsewhere who undertake what they are not able to do. O-p-a-k-e ought to be right, but, like not a few things of which we could argue that they must be right, it happened to be wrong, so what was the use of talking?

11. We heard a little boy in the corner whispering the truth, but afraid as yet to utter it too boldly. It was not the only truth that has appeared first in a whisper. Yet as truth is great and shall prevail, it was but fit that we all finally determined upon o-p-a-q-u-e, and so we did, and we all uttered those letters from all corners of the room with the more perfect confidence as they grew, by each repetition, more familiar to our minds.

LESSON XXI.

BADE (băd), the past tense of *bid*.

BURG′LAR, one who breaks into a dwelling-house at night to rob or harm.

CON′TENTS or CON-TENTS′, that which is contained.

DE-POS′IT (-poz′-), that which is intrusted to another's care.

DE-SIGN′ (de-sīn′ *or* de-zīn′), an intention; a scheme; a sketch.

DES-SERT′ (dez-zert′), a service of fruit after meat.

HARD′EN-ING (härd′n-ing), making or becoming more hard.

KNAV′ER-Y (nāv′er-y), fraud.

LA′BEL, a small slip of writing affixed to a thing.

O-BLIGED′, constrained.

PAR′DON (pär′dn), forgiveness.

POL′I-CY, course of action; art.

PRO-POS′AL (pro-pōz′al), a scheme.

RE-CEIPT′ (re-seet′), a written acknowledgment of money or goods received.

This exercise should be read in those easy colloquial tones which we naturally employ in common conversation. A formal, declamatory tone would be wholly out of place.

THE BREACH OF TRUST.

1. IN the city of New York there lived, not many years ago, two neighbors, one of whom was named Frankheart, and the other Wily. Frank-

heart was too ready to trust every man he met, but Wily loved money so well that he quite forgot that honesty is the best policy. One day Frankheart came into Wily's house, and said: "Neighbor Wily, I am about to make a journey to Ohio to see my uncle, who is very ill. I have five hundred dollars in gold which I want to leave behind. What shall I do with it?"

2. Wily's eyes brightened, and he replied: "I have a good strong iron safe where I keep my money and notes. Fire cannot harm it, and burglars cannot open it. I put the key in a place known only to my wife and myself. I think you cannot do better than keep your gold in my safe." Perhaps Wily had no thought of fraud in his heart at the moment; for he called his wife, and said: "Wife, our neighbor is going to Ohio, and wants to know what he shall do with his gold. I tell him he may put it in our iron safe."

3. "He is quite welcome to do it," said Mrs. Wily, who, in her love of money, was not far behind her husband. "I do not see why his gold would not be as safe there as in the bank. How long shall you be gone, Neighbor Frankheart?" "Only a few weeks, I think," said Frankheart. "I am much obliged to you for your offer to take care of the gold. Here it is"—and producing a bag he emptied the contents on the table—"five hundred dollars in twenty-five pieces of twenty dollars each."

4. He counted the money before their eyes, put

it back in the bag, tied the mouth of it, and called their attention to the written label on it, bearing his name, and showing the amount. Then he gave the bag to Wily, and bade him and his wife good-by. "What a careless man!" said the wife; "he has gone off without taking our receipt for the money." "Of course he trusts to our honor," replied the husband; "we shall not forget it." Wily had not begun to feel the force of temptation.

5. It was nearly a year before Frankheart returned home to New York. From Ohio he had gone to Mexico, and from Mexico to England. The day after his return he called on his neighbors, the Wilys, and said he would trouble them for that little bag of gold. Wily looked at his wife, and his wife at him. Each seemed waiting for the other to speak. At length Wily replied: "Mr. Frankheart, your memory must be failing. It is true you talked of leaving a bag of gold with us, but we gave it back to you, for we did not like to take the risk of having it stolen."

6. "And do *you* say the same?" asked Frankheart, looking at the woman. "Yes," replied she, blushing. "Do you suppose my husband would tell a falsehood? It is not very likely that we would have taken the care of five hundred dollars in gold without being paid for it." "Well, neighbors," said Frankheart, "inasmuch as I omitted to take your receipt for the money, I suppose I must lose it; but you will find that money so got will

not do you much good. I am sorry more for your own sake than for mine. Which do you think will sleep the sounder to-night, you or I?"

7. He took up his hat and left the house, and Mrs. Wily said to her husband: "Call him back, and tell him we were only joking. He's right, husband. The money will be a curse to us." "Oh no, 'tis good shining gold," said Wily; "besides, Frankheart is much richer than we are. He can afford to lose it." Frankheart went to Judge Brown, and told him the story. "And did you take a receipt for the money?" asked the judge. "No," replied Frankheart; "I supposed Neighbor Wily was honest as the sun, and then his wife stood by, and saw me give him the gold."

8. "Well, Mr. Frankheart, do you step into that inner room and wait, while I send for this Mr. Wily and question him." Frankheart obeyed, and the judge sent an officer to request Wily to call at the judge's office without delay. As soon as Wily arrived, the judge said to him: "I learn that you have received as a deposit a large sum of money in gold, and that you refuse to return it to the right owner. What do you say to the charge?" "I deny it wholly," replied Wily.

9. "Well," replied Judge Brown, "let us suppose you innocent; but, in order to convince me of it, write to your wife the letter I am about to dictate to you. She is said to have been a witness to the transaction, and if what you say is true it

can be easily shown. Now, sir, write these words." "But, may it please your honor," said Wily, who was not well pleased at the proposal, "why not let me go home and bring my wife before you? That will be the most direct way of learning what she has to say." "Allow me to choose my own way," said the judge. "Here are pen, ink and paper. Write!"

10. Wily looked at the door, as if he were half inclined to run; but as officers stood near, that plan was not to be thought of. He took up a pen and wrote, while the judge dictated these words: "My dear wife: Give the bearer that bag of gold belonging to Mr. Frankheart. I am about to restore it to him." The judge carefully examined the letter to see that it contained these words and nothing more. Wily rose to go, hoping he might reach his home in season to explain matters to his wife; but the judge, in a loud, stern voice, exclaimed, "Sit down, sir, and wait for the return of my messenger."

11. Trembling at the thought of exposure, Wily sank into a chair. One of the officers received from the judge the letter and departed. In less than half an hour the officer returned with a bag, which he gave to the judge, who read the label, and then counted the money, and found that it amounted to just five hundred dollars. The wretched Wily threw himself on his knees, confessed his knavery, and begged the judge to forgive him. The judge threw open a door, and pointing to Frankheart,

said to Wily, "Here is the man to whom you must sue for pardon."

12. "I think, judge," said Mr. Frankheart, "that his own conscience will punish him enough." "I am not sure of that," replied the judge; "men capable of such baseness have generally succeeded in hardening and perverting what little conscience they may have had. But if you refuse to appear against this man, he can be released." "I do refuse," said Frankheart, "for I hope he will reform." "Then," said the judge, "I have nothing more to say, except that you, Mr. Frankheart, deserve to be rebuked for trusting any man, honest or dishonest, with money, without taking a receipt." Having spoken these words, the judge dismissed them.

LESSON XXII.

Dis′so-lute, loose; vicious.
Frail′ty, weakness; liability to error.
Gain-say′, to contradict.
Ma-tur′i-ty, ripeness; full age.
Ne′er (nār), contraction of *never.*
Pal′ter (pawl′ter), to shift or dodge; to quibble.
Re-pulsed′, beat back; checked.
Sol′ace, comfort; relief.

NO.

I.

There's a word very short, but decided and plain,
  That speaks to the purpose at once;
Not a child but its meaning can quickly explain,
  Yet often 'tis hard to pronounce.
What a world of vexation and trouble 'twould spare,
  What peace and content 'twould bestow,

If we turned, when temptation would lure and ensnare,
  And firmly repulsed it with "No!"

II.

When the idler would tempt us, with trifles and play,
  To waste the bright moments so dear,
When the scoffer unholy our faith would gainsay,
  And mock at the word we revere,
When dissolute folly and sin would invite,
  And a snare over conscience would throw,
Never palter with truth for a fleeting delight,
  But check the first impulse with "No!"

III.

In the morning of life, in maturity's day,
  Whatever the cares that engage,
Be the precepts of virtue our guide and our stay,
  Our solace from childhood to age!
Thus the heart shall not waver, no matter how tried,
  But firmness and constancy show,
And when passion or frailty would draw us aside,
  We'll spurn the seducer with "No!"

LESSON XXIII.

COM′BAT (kŏm′- *or* kŭm′-), a fight.
EX-AS′PER-AT-ED (ĕgz-), provoked.
FE-RO′CIOUS, fierce; wild.
HUMBLE (hŭm′bl or ŭm′bl), lowly.
LA′MA or LLA′MA (lā′ma), a small species of camel.
MEN-AG′E-RIE (mĕn-ăzh′ĕ-ry), a place where wild beasts are kept.
NOOSE (nooz or noos), a running knot.
RAFT′ER, a roof-timber.
SAGACIOUS (să-gā′shus), quick of scent; shrewd; acute; intelligent.
SAV′AGE, fierce; ĭnhuman.
TI′GRESS, female of the tiger.

SCENE IN A MENAGERIE.

1. NOT long since, in a menagerie of wild animals, a tigress broke out of her cage during the

absence of the keeper at dinner. The ferocious beast sprang at a lama, killed it, and was sucking its blood when the keeper entered.

2. The man's first attempt was to fling a noose over the head of the tigress, but before he could do this she turned and prepared to spring. It was a moment of extreme peril.

3. The eyes of the tigress flashed fire, and her opened jaws threatened death. The keeper knew not what to do. He had but a moment in which to decide. In that moment he darted behind an elephant which stood near by.

4. The sagacious animal seemed to comprehend what was going on. He was calm but vigilant. The tigress, raising herself on her hind feet, sprang with her utmost force, and was bounding by in pursuit of the keeper, when the elephant put forth his trunk, seized the furious beast and pitched her to the farther end of the apartment.

5. All the animals were by this time in a state of commotion. The monkeys jumped for their lives, and scattered wildly. The baboons scampered up the rafters and there held on, looking down and winking at the enraged tigress as she rose from her fall. The elephant maintained his composure, and the lion looked on with dignity from his cage.

6. The savage tigress seemed resolved not to give up the combat. She was creeping along as if to renew the attack, when the keeper thought he would get on the elephant's back, and commanded

him to place him there. This the sagacious animal did with a single toss of his trunk.

7. The tigress was exasperated at seeing the man thus put out of her reach. She drew back and made another spring at him, but the elephant caught her midway, and hurled her with great force against the wall. Bruised and humbled, she gave up the fight after this, and slunk back quietly into her cage without doing any more mischief.

THE FLOWERS OF THE FIELD.

YOUR voiceless lips, O flowers, are living preachers,
  Each cup a pulpit, and each leaf a book,
Supplying to my fancy numerous teachers
      From loneliest nook.

Floral apostles! that in dewy splendor
  Weep without woe, and blush without a crime!
Oh may I deeply learn, and ne'er surrender,
      Your lore sublime!

LESSON XXIV.

dunce	drone	white	break′fast
once	scold	night	pleas′ant

THE TARDY BOY.

MOTHER.

SEE! the hour for school is near:
Robert, Robert, do you hear?

ROBERT.

Mother, mother, do not fret!
I'm not through my breakfast yet.

MOTHER.

From your bed you should have sprung
When the early bell was rung.

ROBERT.

All my window-panes were white
With the frost we had last night.

MOTHER.

If you would not be a dunce,
Brave the cold, and rise at once.

ROBERT.

When Jack Frost is in the case,
Bed is such a pleasant place!

MOTHER.

He who loves his bed so well
Never, never will excel.

ROBERT.

Mother, mother, do not scold!
I shall soon be eight years old.

MOTHER.

More's the shame for you, my son,
Leaving duties thus undone!

ROBERT.

Something whispers in my ear,
You are right, my mother dear.

MOTHER.

Then get down, sir, from your stool,
And run quickly off to school.

ROBERT.

Off I go! you shall not see
After this a drone in me.

LESSON XXV.

COL-LO'QUI-AL, conversational.
COM'PASS (kŭm-), space; an instrument by which ships are steered.
DOESN'T, a contraction of *does not.*
E'QUA-BLY, evenly; uniformly.
EX-TRAOR'DI-NA-RY (eks-tror-), uncommon; remarkable.
FRIV'O-LOUS, slight; vain.
HAUNT (hänt), to resort to.
MA-RINE' (ma-reen'), of the sea.
OF-FI'CIOUS (fish'us), meddling.
PROG'RESS, motion forward.
WRITH'ING (rīth'ing), twisting with violence or pain.
YOU'RE, contraction of *you are.*

BREVITIES.

EXERCISES IN COLLOQUIAL DELIVERY.

1. HOW TO RUIN HEALTH.—A humorous writer gives the following rules for ruining health: Stay in bed late. Eat hot suppers. Turn day into night, and night into day. Take no exercise. Always ride when you can walk. Never mind about wet feet. Have half a dozen doctors. Take all the medicine they give you. Try every new quack. If that doesn't kill you, quack yourself.

2. CARRYING A JOKE TOO FAR.—A fellow stole a saw, and on his trial told the judge that he only took it in joke. "How far did you carry it?" inquired the judge. "Two miles," answered the prisoner. "Ah! that's carrying a joke too far!" said the judge, and the prisoner was sentenced to hard labor in the house of correction for three months.

3. TOO OFFICIOUS.—"Your house is on fire!" exclaimed a stranger, rushing into the parlor of a pompous and formal citizen. "Well, sir," replied the latter, "to what cause am I indebted for the

extraordinary interest which you seem to take in the affairs of my house?"

4. MAKING THE BEST OF THINGS.—"I have told you," says a celebrated poet, "of the Spaniard who, when about to eat cherries, always put on spectacles, in order that the fruit might look larger and more tempting. In like manner I make the most of my enjoyments, and though I do not cast my eyes away from my troubles, I pack them in as small a compass as I can for myself, and never let them annoy others."

5. FATE OF IDLERS.—The man who did not think it was respectable to bring up his children to work has just heard from his three sons. One of them is a driver on a canal, another has been taken up as a vagrant, and the third has gone to a certain public institution to learn to hammer stone under a keeper.

6. THE DULL RAZOR.—"Does this razor go easy?" asked a barber of his customer, who was writhing under a clumsy instrument, the chief recommendation of which was a strong handle. "Well," replied the poor fellow, "that depends on what you call this operation. If you're skinning me, the razor goes tolerably easy, but if you're shaving me, it goes rather hard." "Doesn't it take hold?" asked the barber. "Yes, it takes hold, but it won't let go," replied the victim.

7. MURDERING A TUNE.—Foote once asked a man without a sense of tune in him, "Why are you for ever humming that tune?" "Because it

haunts me," was the reply. "No wonder," said Foote; "you are for ever murdering it."

8. THE QUAKER'S RETORT.—A Quaker and a hot-headed youth were, on a recent occasion, quarreling in the street. The man with the broad-brimmed hat kept his temper most equably, which seemed but to increase the anger of the other. "Fellow," said the latter with an oath, "I don't know a bigger fool than you are." "Stop, friend," replied the Quaker; "thou dost forget thyself."

9. ON EARLY RISING.—Said Lord Chatham to his son: "I would inscribe on the curtains of your bed and the walls of your chamber, 'If you do not rise early, you can make progress in nothing. If you do not set apart your hours of reading, if you suffer yourself or any one else to break in upon them, your days will slip through your hands unprofitable and frivolous, and unenjoyed by yourself.'"

10. THE JUDGE AND THE LAWYER.—On a certain occasion, when pleading a cause at the bar, Lawyer Brooks observed to Judge Rice that he would conclude his remarks on the following day unless the court would consent to *set* late enough for him to finish them that evening. "*Sit*, sir," said the judge, "not *set:* hens set." "I stand corrected, sir," replied the lawyer, bowing. Not long after, the judge, while giving an opinion in a marine case, asked, in regard to a certain ship, "At what wharf does she *lay?*" "*Lie*, may it please your honor," exclaimed Mr. Brooks, "not *lay:* hens lay."

LESSON XXVI.

A-POTH′E-CA-RY, one who dispenses medicines.

BE-STOW′AL, act of giving.

DIS-AS′TER, misfortune; grief.

PAST′URE, land on which cattle feed.

RAIL′LER-Y (răl′ler-y), banter, slight ridicule; irony.

RES′CUED, set free; delivered.

TAUNT (tänt), an insult.

VAUNT (vänt), a boast; a brag.

WOUND′ED (woond′ed), hurt.

THE PRIZE FOR HEROISM.

1. IT was the day of a public exhibition at our academy. A number of ladies and gentlemen, the parents and friends of the scholars, were present. Prizes for scholarship had been awarded to a number of boys, and much applause had been bestowed upon some of those who had excelled in declamation.

2. At last our teacher stood up and remarked that there was one prize, consisting of a gold medal, which was rarely awarded, not so much on account of its great cost as because the instances were rare which rendered its bestowal proper. It was the prize for heroism. The last boy who received it was young Manners, who, three years ago, at the risk of his own life, rescued a child from drowning.

3. "With the permission of this company," said the teacher, "I will now relate a brief story. Not long since, some boys of this school were flying a kite in the street just as a poor lad on horseback rode by on his way to mill. The horse took fright and threw the lad, injuring him so that he was carried home and confined some weeks to his bed. Of the boys who had caused the disaster, none followed to learn the fate of the wounded lad. There was one boy of this school, however, who had witnessed the accident from a distance, who not only went to make inquiries, but stayed to render services.

4. "This boy soon learned that the wounded lad was the grandson of a poor widow whose sole means of support consisted in selling the milk of a fine cow of which she was the owner. What could she do now? She was old and lame, and her grandson, on whom she had depended to drive the cow to pasture, was on his back helpless. 'Never mind, good woman,' said the boy of the academy; 'I can drive your cow.' With blessings and thanks the old woman accepted his offer.

5. "But his kindness did not stop here. Money was wanted to get articles from the apothecary. 'I have some money that my mother sent me to buy a pair of boots with,' said our scholar, 'but I can do without them for a while.' 'Oh no,' said the old woman, 'I can't consent to that; but here is a new pair of cow-hide boots that I bought for Henry, who now can't wear them. If you would only buy these, giving us what they cost, we should get along nicely.' The scholar bought the boots, clumsy as they were, and has worn them up to this time.

6. "Well, when it was discovered by other boys of the academy that our scholar was in the habit of driving a cow, he was assailed by them every day with laughter and ridicule. 'Admire those boots!' one boy would cry; 'the latest Paris style!' 'What's the price of milk?' would be the taunt of another; and, 'How much water do you put in the cans, Jonathan?'

7. "To all these jeers our scholar presented a brave and cheerful front, driving the widow's cow and wearing his thick boots without a word of explanation, for he was not inclined to make a vaunt of his charitable motives, and, furthermore, in his heart, he had no sympathy with the false pride that could look with ridicule on any useful employment. It was by mere accident that his course of kindness and self-denial was yesterday made known to his teacher.

8. "And now, ladies and gentlemen, I appeal to

you if there was not true heroism in this boy's conduct. Nay, Master Hartley, do not slink out of sight behind the blackboard! You were not afraid of ridicule: you must not now be afraid of praise. Come forth, come forth, Master Edward James Hartley, and let us see your honest face. You need not be ashamed of it."

9. As Hartley, with blushing cheeks, made his appearance, what a round of applause, in which the whole company joined, spoke the general approbation of his conduct! The ladies stood up on benches and waved their handkerchiefs. The old men wiped the gathering moisture from the corners of their eyes and clapped their hands. Those clumsy boots on Hartley's feet seemed a prouder ornament than a crown would have been on his head. The medal was bestowed on him amid general acclamation, in which all the boys, including those who had once laughed at him, now heartily joined.

10. One of them, of the name of Jameson, went up after we were dismissed, and with the tears of a manly self-rebuke in his eyes tendered his hand to Hartley, and made a handsome apology for his past insolence and ill-manners. "Think no more of it, old fellow," said Hartley, with delightful cordiality; "let us all go and have a good ramble in the woods before we break up for vacation." The boys, one by one, followed Jameson's example, and then we set forth with huzzas into the woods. What a happy day it was!

LESSON XXVII.

CA-REER′, a course; a race.

CHAR-AC-TER-IS′TIC, peculiar; constituting or marking character.

CON′SCIENCE, the faculty of knowing right and wrong.

COW′ERED, sank by bending the knees; crouched.

DIS-CERN′ (diz-zern′), to make distinction.

EAR′NEST, zealous; serious.

EX-POUND′ER, an explainer.

I-DE′AL, existing in idea.

IM-PLIC′IT (-plis′it), firm; implied; resting on authority of others.

IN-GEN′U-OUS (-jen′-), frank.

NEU′TRAL, indifferent.

PLI′ANT, easily bent.

PRAC′TICE or PRAC′TISE, to perform constantly; to do habitually.

PRIS′TINE (pris′tĭn), first; earliest.

RO-MANCE′, a tale of wild adventure.

RUG′BY, a market-town in the center of England.

TEM′PO-RAL, relating to time and to things of the world.

ZEST, relish; flavor.

ARNOLD THE TEACHER.

1. THE career of Thomas Arnold, the distinguished instructor of youth, though teeming with the poetry of common life, was not one of stirring incident or romance: it consisted in laboring to his best in his sacred vocation. Born in England in 1795, he was educated at Winchester College, and in 1827 became head-master of Rugby School. He died in 1842 at the early age of forty-seven.

2. His professional life began at Rugby, and he plunged into fourteen years of uninterrupted toil. Holding labor to be his appointed lot on earth, he harnessed himself cheerfully to his work. A craving for rest was to him a sure sign that neither mind nor body retained its pristine vigor, and he determined, while blessed with health, to proceed

like the camel in the wilderness, and die with his burden on his back. His characteristic trait was intense earnestness. He felt life keenly, its responsibilities as well as its enjoyments. His very pleasures were earnest. In nothing was he indifferent or neutral.

3. His principles were few: the fear of God was the beginning of his wisdom, and his object was not so much to teach knowledge as the means of acquiring it—to furnish, in a word, the key to the temple. He desired to awaken the intellect of each individual boy, and contended that the main movement must come from *within*, and not from *without* the pupil, and that all that *could* be should be done *by* him, and not *for* him.

4. In a word, his scheme was to call forth in the little world of school those capabilities which best fitted boys for their career in the great world. He was not only possessed of strength, but had the art of imparting it; he had the power to grasp a subject himself, and then ingraft it on the intellect of others.

5. His pupils were made to feel that there was a work for them to do—that their happiness as well as their duty lay in doing that work well. Hence an indescribable zest was communicated to a young man's feeling about life; a strange joy came over him on discerning that he had the means of being useful, and thus of being happy. He was inspired with a humble, profound and most religious consciousness that work is the appointed calling of

man on earth, the element in which his nature is ordained to develop itself, and in which his progressive advancement toward heaven is to lie.

6. The three ends at which Arnold aimed, in the order of their relative importance, were, first and foremost, to inculcate religious and moral principle, then gentlemanlike conduct, and, lastly, intellectual ability. To his mind, religion and politics—the doing one's duty to God and to man—were the two things really wanting. Unlike the schoolmasters of his early life, he held all the scholarship man ever had, to be infinitely worthless in comparison with even a very humble degree of spiritual advancement.

7. He loved tuition for itself, of which he fully felt the solemn responsibility and the ideal beauty, and which he was among the first to elevate to its true dignity. It was the destiny and business of his entire life. His own youthfulness of temperament and vigor fitted him better for the society of the young than of the old; he enjoyed their spring of mind and body, and by personal intercourse hoped to train up and mold to good their pliant minds while wax to receive and marble to retain.

8. He led his pupils to place implicit trust in his decisions, and to esteem his approbation as their highest reward. He gained his end by treating them as gentlemen, as reasonable beings, in whose conscience and common sense he might confide; and to this appeal to their nobler faculties, to his

relying on their honor, the ingenuous youth responded worthily.

9. Once, when teaching a rather dull boy, he spoke somewhat sharply to him, on which the pupil looked up in his face, and said, "Why do you speak so angrily, sir? *Indeed*, I am doing the best I can." Arnold at once acknowledged his error, and expressed his regret for it. Years afterward he used to tell the story to his children, and added, "I never felt so much in my life: that look and that speech I have never forgotten."

10. One of his principal holds was in his boy-sermons—that is, in sermons to which his young congregation could and did listen, and of which he was the absolute inventor. The secret of that power lay in its intimate connection with the man himself. He spoke with both spiritual and temporal authority, and truths divine seemed mended by the tongue of an expounder whose discourse was a living one—doctrine in action—and where precept was enforced by example.

11. His was the exhibition of a simple, earnest man, who practiced what he preached, who probed the depths of life, and expressed strongly and plainly his love of goodness and abhorrence of sin. There was, indeed, a moral supremacy in him; his eyes looked into the heart, and all that was base and mean cowered before him, and, when he preached, a sympathetic thrill ran through his audience. His was the eloquence which goes swiftly to the heart of every hearer.

LESSON XXVIII.

BEACON (bē'kn), a signal-fire.
CHORUS (kō'rus), verses of a song in which the company join.
CHURL, a surly, ill-bred fellow.
COR'O-NAL, a wreath or crown.
DROSS, scum; worldly riches.
DROUGHTY (drow'ty), dry; arid.
HYMNLESS (hĭm'lĕs), having or singing no hymn.
LUSCIOUS (lŭsh'ŭs), very sweet.
LUST'Y, strong; vigorous.
NE'ER (nār), a contraction of *never*
NIG'GARD, a miser.
PER-FUME', to scent.
SCANT'Y, small; narrow.
TRANS-PORT'ED, carried away affected with delight.
WORLD'LING, a worldly person.

"NOT TO MYSELF ALONE."

I.

"NOT to myself alone,"
The little opening flower transported cries—
"Not to myself alone I bud and bloom;
With fragrant breath the breezes I perfume,
And gladden all things with my rainbow dies.
The bee comes sipping, every eventide,
His dainty fill;
The butterfly within my cup doth hide
From threatening ill."

II.

"Not to myself alone,"
The circling star with honest pride doth boast—
"Not to myself alone I rise and set;
I write upon night's coronal of jet
His power and skill who formed our myriad host;
A friendly beacon at heaven's open gate,
I gem the sky,
That man might ne'er forget, in every fate,
His home on high."

III.

"Not to myself alone,"
The heavy-laden bee doth murmuring hum—
"Not to myself alone, from flower to flower,
I rove the wood, the garden and the bower,
And to the hive at evening weary come:
For man, for man, the luscious food I pile
With busy care,
Content if he repay my ceaseless toil
With scanty share."

IV.

"Not to myself alone,"
The soaring bird with lusty pinion sings—
"Not to myself alone I raise my song;
I cheer the drooping with my warbling tongue,
And bear the mourner on my viewless wings;
I bid the hymnless churl my anthem learn,
And God adore;
I call the worldling from his dross to turn,
And sing and soar."

V.

"Not to myself alone,"
The streamlet whispers on its pebbly way—
"Not to myself alone I sparkling glide;
I scatter health and life on every side,
And strew the fields with herb and floweret gay
I sing unto the common bleak and bare
My gladsome tune;
I sweeten and refresh the languid air
In droughty June."

VI.

"Not to myself alone!"
O man, forget not thou—earth's honored priest,

Its tongue, its soul, its life, its pulse, its heart—
In earth's great chorus to sustain *thy* part!
Chiefest of guests at Love's ungrudging feast,
Play not the niggard; spurn thy native clod,
And *self* disown;
Live to thy neighbor; live unto thy God:
Not to thyself alone!

LESSON XXIX.

AN'SWERED, responded to.
HEART'Y, cordial; robust.
KIN'DLINGS, materials for making a fire.
SNEER'ING, scoffing; jeering.
SHOV'EL (shuv'vl), to throw with a shovel.
SHRINK'ING, drawing back.

THAT'S HOW.

1. IT was a bitter cold day. There had been a great snow-storm, and the sky still had a black and angry look. "Dear me!" said Mrs. Wilson

as she glanced out of the window; "the doorways are all blocked up; see how the snow has drifted into the yard! Ann cannot get out to the wood-shed for her kindlings. Those poor hens, too, have not been fed since yesterday morning. What shall we do without somebody to dig a path for us!"

2. "I can shovel a path, grandmother," said John, a bright boy about eight years old. "It is too hard work for you, I fear," said Mrs. Wilson; "and besides, we have nothing but this coal-sifter to shovel with." "No matter," said John; "I can try."

3. So he put on his hat, tied his tippet round his neck, turned up his trowsers, and went to work with a will. But while he was tossing away the snow, a man with a pipe in his mouth and his hands in his pockets came lounging along.

4. Instead of lending John a helping hand or saying to him a kind word, as such a great hearty fellow might have done, he called out in a sneering tone, "Boy, why don't you get a spoon to shovel with? How do you expect to get through that snow-drift with that thing?"

5. "By keeping at it—that's how!" answered John, looking up and letting the snow fall from his little coal-sifter. Then, without wasting any more time in words, he turned to his work again. Hard work it was. He was soon very tired and his back began to ache. But he kept at his task bravely until he had dug a good path.

6. Now, girls and boys, we all shall have paths

to dig of one kind or another as we go through life. Many snow-drifts will lie in our way. But if we will all keep at work with a good heart, we shall be sure to come out right at last. Bear this in mind; and when you find yourselves shrinking from any useful labor, and asking yourselves, "How shall I ever do this?" be ready with John Wilson's answer, "By keeping at it—that's how!"

LESSON XXX.

AN′CHOR (ăng′kur), an iron to hold a ship in the water.

COM′PASS (kum′pass), an instrument for determining horizontal directions.

GLIS′TEN-ING (glis′sn-ing), glittering.

HA′VEN (ha′vn), a bay; a harbor.

PIV′OT, a pin or point on which anything turns.

PROP′ER-TY, a peculiar quality; a possession.

VIS′I-BLE, that may be seen.

THE COMPASS.

1. A PERSON does not need to go to sea in order to find out how lost and helpless a sailor would be in the midst of the ocean if he had no compass.

A few summers ago I passed some days at one of the Isles of Shoals, a small rocky group in the Atlantic Ocean, ten miles from the coast of New Hampshire, and I used to go out almost every day in a boat, fishing for cod and haddock.

2. One misty morning, I remember, I started with three or four others for one of the favorite fishing places, about half a mile off. We had been there for an hour or two, and had caught a few very fine fish, when some one, looking up, cried out, "Where is the island?"

3. We all looked around, but the island was gone. The mist had changed into a dense fog, which had gathered over our rocky abode, and hid it completely from our view. Nor was there any object in sight, except another of the island boats, containing a fishing-party like ourselves. We called out to them, "Where is the island?" To which one of them replied, "It has drifted out to sea." Which, in fact, *we* might have done, if we had been a little farther off.

4. I cannot tell you how entirely lost we seemed for a few minutes. Every one gave his opinion as to the direction in which the island was; but as our boat had been floating about without an anchor, and had consequently changed its position every moment, it was all guess-work, and we might have rowed about for a whole day without finding the object of our search.

5. While we were talking the matter over, we heard the large bell of the hotel ring, which of

course told us the way we were to go, in order to reach the island. So we kept on our fishing for two or three hours longer, and the mist soon rolled away, revealing to view the gray rock, the long white hotel, the ladies walking about, and the little boys fishing for perch along the shore.

6. We afterward learned that the regular frequenters of this island considered it unsafe to go a hundred yards from the shore without a compass, and always took a pocket-compass with them in case a sudden fog should wrap the island from their sight.

7. Admirable invention! I often wonder that a thing so valuable can be so small, simple and cheap. It is nothing but a needle, a pivot and a card, which you can buy for half a dollar, and carry it in your pocket, or dangle it at the end of a watch-chain. Yet, small and trifling as it is, a ship's company that should find themselves in the middle of the ocean without a compass would consider it a great favor to be allowed to buy one for many thousand dollars.

8. But stop; some of the young folks who live far from the sea coast, and have never seen the magnetic needle quivering in its box under its glass lid, may not know exactly what a compass is. Well, you must know there is a kind of iron ore, of a dark gray color, found in iron mines in many parts of the world, which is called loadstone, or natural magnet. It is about as heavy as the

common iron ore, and looks like it, except that it is a little more glistening.

9. It has, however, most wonderful and mysterious properties. One is, that it attracts to itself iron and other metals. Another property of the magnet is equally mysterious and far more important to man. If you take a bar of iron or steel, and rub it against a loadstone, and then suspend it carefully in the middle by a thread, it will always point north and south, or very nearly north and south. Now, a compass is nothing more than a small steel needle, which, having been rubbed against a magnet in a certain manner, is balanced with great nicety upon a pivot, and the whole inclosed in a box.

10. That needle points toward the North Star, and serves to guide the mariner over the trackless deep when neither sun nor star is visible. It does not tell him where he is, but it tells him in what direction he is sailing, and it tells him, with the help of other instruments, in what direction he must sail to reach the haven where he would be.

INVOCATION.

FATHER of light and life! thou Good Supreme!
Oh, teach *me* what is good! teach me thyself!
Save me from folly, vanity and vice,
From every low pursuit; and feed my soul
With knowledge, conscious peace, and virtue pure—
Sacred, substantial, never-fading bliss!

LESSON XXXI.

FAWN, a young deer.

FELICIA HEMANS, author of this spirited poem, was born in Liverpool, England, 1793, died 1835.

GAL′LANT, brave; fine.

IN′DIAN (ind′yan or in′di-an), a native of India; an aboriginal inhabitant of America.

SHIV′ER, to quake; to tremble.

THE CAPTIVE'S DREAM.

I.

I DREAM of all things free!
  Of a gallant, gallant bark
That sweeps through storm and sea
  Like an arrow to its mark!
Of a stag that o'er the hills
  Goes bounding in his glee;
Of a thousand flashing rills,
  Of all things glad and free.

II.

I dream of some proud bird,
  A bright-eyed mountain king:
In my visions I have heard
  The rushing of his wing;
I follow some wild river
  On whose breast no sail may be;
Dark woods around it shiver:
  I dream of all things free;

III.

Of a happy forest child,
  With the fawns and flowers at play;
Of an Indian 'mid the wild,
  With the stars to guide his way;
Of a chief his warriors leading,
  Of an archer's greenwood tree;
My heart in chains is bleeding,
  And I dream of all things free!

LESSON XXXII.

AC-CU-MU-LA′TION, the act of heaping up.
AR′GU-MENT, a reason offered.
COPE, to strive; to match.
E-LEC′TION, choice.
EN-TREAT′Y, urgent prayer.
EX-TEN′U-ATE, to lessen; to excuse.
FOR′MI-DA-BLE, fearful.
IN-EV′I-TA-BLE, not to be shunned.
IN-VIN′CI-BLE, not to be conquered.
MAR′TIAL (-shal), warlike.
PE-TI′TION, a formal request.
REC-ON-CIL-I-A′TION, renewal of friendship.
RE-MON′STRANCE, strong advice against a thing.
RIV′ET, to fasten with rivets.
VIG′I-LANT (vij′-), watchful.

Sound the *h* in humble and exhausted. Pronounce none, *nŭn;* were, *wer;* been, *bĭn;* against, *agĕnst;* parliament, *par′le-ment.* Do not say *bruthren* for brĕth′ren; *fŏrging* for fōrging.

SPEECH OF PATRICK HENRY.*

1. I ASK, gentlemen, what means this martial array, if its purpose be not to force us to submission? Can gentlemen assign any other possible motive for it? Has Great Britain any enemy in this quarter of the world to call for all this accumulation of navies and armies? No, sir, she has none. They are meant for us; they can be meant for no other; they are sent over to bind and rivet upon us those chains which the British ministry have been so long forging.

2. And what have we to oppose them? Shall we try argument? Sir, we have been trying that for the last ten years. Have we anything new to offer upon the subject? Nothing. Shall we resort

* Patrick Henry, a native of Virginia, was born 1736, died 1799. The speech from which the above extract is made was delivered March 23, 1775, in the Virginia Convention.

to entreaty and humble supplication? What terms shall we find which have not been already exhausted? We have petitioned—we have remonstrated—we have supplicated—we have prostrated ourselves before the throne, and have implored its interposition to arrest the tyrannical hands of the ministry and parliament.

3. Our petitions have been slighted; our remonstrances have produced additional violence and insult; our supplications have been disregarded; and we have been spurned with contempt from the foot of the throne. In vain, after these things, may we indulge the fond hope of peace and reconciliation. There is no longer any room for hope. If we wish to be free, we must fight! I repeat it, sir, we must fight. An appeal to arms and to the God of hosts is all that is left us.

4. They tell us that we are weak, unable to cope with so formidable an adversary. But when shall we be stronger? Will it be the next week, or the next year? Will it be when we are totally disarmed, and when a British guard shall be stationed in every house? Sir, we are not weak, if we make a proper use of those means in our power. Three millions of people, armed in the holy cause of liberty, and in such a country as that which we possess, are invincible by any force which our enemy can send against us.

5. Besides, sir, we shall not fight our battles alone. There is a just Being who presides over the destinies of nations, and who will raise up

friends to fight our battles for us. The battle, sir, is not to the strong alone: it is to the vigilant, the active, the brave. Besides, sir, we have no election. If we were base enough to desire it, it is now too late to retire from the contest. There is no retreat but in submission and slavery.

6. Our chains are forged. Their clanking may be heard on the plains of Boston. The war is inevitable—and let it come! I repeat it, sir, let it come! It is vain to extenuate the matter. Gentlemen may cry, Peace, peace, but there is no peace. The war is actually begun! The next gale that sweeps from the North will bring to our ears the clash of resounding arms. Our brethren are already in the field.

7. Why stand we here idle? What is it that gentlemen wish? What would they have? Is life so dear, or peace so sweet, as to be purchased at the price of chains and slavery! Forbid it, Heaven! I know not what course others may take, but as for me, give me liberty or give me death!

BE BRAVE, BE JUST.

Be brave, be just; and, when your country's laws
Call you to witness in a dubious cause,
Though power should plant his rack before your eye
And, frowning, dictate to your lips the lie,
Think it a crime no tears can e'er efface
To purchase safety with compliance base,
At honor's cost a feverish span extend,
And sacrifice for life life's only end!

LESSON XXXIII.

AN'I-MAT-ED, having life.

CIR-CUM'FER-ENCE, a line that bounds the space of a circle.

DI-AM'E-TER, distance through the center, as of a circle.

GIRTH, a band encircling.

IN-QUIR'IES, questions.

LEARN'ED, knowing; well informed.

LEV'EL, horizontal; flat.

SAT'EL-LITE, a small or secondary planet; an attendant.

SUS'TE-NANCE, that which sustains life.

TEL'E-SCOPE, an instrument for viewing distant objects.

TWINK'LING, sparkling at intervals.

THE EARTH AND THE STARS.

1. IT seems strange that it is not a level surface which we stand upon, but a globe shaped somewhat like an orange. The firm earth beneath our feet is nothing else than a large ball—so large that the greatest extent of surface which the eye can see at one time appears quite flat.

2. To assure ourselves that the earth is round, we may, on a clear day, look out from some high

ground upon the ocean, when we shall see the tops of approaching vessels first appear, and gradually the lower parts. The earth is about eight thousand miles in diameter or thickness, so that its circumference or girth is twenty-five thousand miles.

3. Nearly three-fourths of its surface is covered with water, forming seas and oceans. The re-

mainder is very irregular, presenting hills and ranges of mountains, with valleys, slopes and plains. The land is covered with a great variety of herbs and trees, and inhabited by many kinds of animals. Races of men, either in a civilized or savage condition, occupy much of the surface.

4. Although the earth may seem very large, it is, after all, only the third of a set or system of globes, called planets, which move at different distances in space round the sun, and all of which are supposed to be occupied by living beings and the things necessary for their sustenance.

5. The moon is a small globe which moves in like manner round the earth, and some of the other planets have moons or satellites moving round them. The sun, which gives light and heat to the planets, is a body of vast size—one million four hundred thousand times larger than the earth.

6. The earth is distant from the sun ninety-five millions of miles, and the last, or most distant of the planets as yet discovered, is not nearer than three thousand six hundred millions of miles. If there were a road from the earth to the sun, and a man were to ride along that road at the rate of a mile in the minute, which was the speed of the swiftest horse ever known, he would require a hundred and eighty years, or two long lifetimes, to perform the journey.

7. Great as is the space occupied by the sun and planets, it is but a small portion of the universe.

Every little star which is seen twinkling in the sky is a sun like ours, supposed to be surrounded, too, with a similar system of planets, which, like our earth, are the residences of animated creatures. Though the stars seem near to each other, they are in reality millions of millions of miles apart.

8. Nor do we see all. When we look through a telescope, which is an instrument for bringing within our sight objects too distant to be seen with the naked eye, we discover many stars, and we always bring more into view, the greater power we give the telescope. The number of the stars is indeed beyond all calculation.

9. What is here stated has been made quite certain by the inquiries of learned men, but we have not yet, apparently, comprehended the whole of nature. There is reason for supposing that the stars which we see by means of the naked eye and the telescope form but one cluster of earths moving in space.

10. Far beyond the bounds of that vast cluster, astronomers have perceived similar clusters of worlds, made to appear small by being so far off that most of them look like clouds of faint light upon the dark ground of the sky. Indeed, it is as impossible to conceive a limit to space as to the power of the Creator.

QUESTIONS.—What is the shape of this earth on which we live? How can we assure ourselves that the earth is round? What do you understand by the diameter of a globe? By the circumference? What is estimated to be the diameter of the earth in miles?

LESSON XXXIV.

AC-QUAINT′ANCE, fellowship.
CLOTHES (klōthz *or* klōz), coverings of cloth.
COL′UMN (kol′um), a perpendicular row of words; a pillar.
DEF-I-NI′TION, explanation.
DIF′FER-ENT, unlike; distinct.
GRAT-I-FI-CA′TION, high satisfaction.
HON′OR-A-BLE, worthy of honor upright; just; fair.
HOST′LER (hos′ler), one who has the care of horses.
IN′TER-EST, concern; advantage.
SKATE, to move with skates.
SO-LIL′O-QUY, a talking to one's self.
SPOIL, to injure; to deface.

THE TWO SOLILOQUIES.

Soliloquy of the Idle Boy.

1. DEAR me! what a trouble it is to learn lessons and to go to school! Here I have one, two —no, not two, but a column and a half, of words with meanings, to get by heart. Well, I suppose I must begin to learn them: p-r-i-s pris, o-n on,

prison, "a place where people are confined." Why couldn't they say a *school*, at once? What worse prison can there be than that?

2. Well, well; what comes next? P-u-n pun, i-s-h ish, punish. I know the meaning of that word without looking at the book—I hear it so often. "Charles," says mother, "if you *will* spoil your clothes in this manner, I shall ask your father to punish you." "Charles," says the housemaid, "you deserve to be punished for bringing in so much mud on your shoes."

3. Oh, this ugly lesson! I never shall get it! P-l-e-a-s pleas, u-r-e ure, pleasure, "gratification of mind." Pooh! I can give a much better definition of pleasure than that. Pleasure means swinging on gates, eating candy, shooting robins, playing at hide-and-seek, flying a kite, having a high time. I dare say, if Charles Knight heard me, he would say pleasure means having a new book.

4. Read, read, read—I hate reading. When I am a man, I'll never open a book, and I'll never send my children to school, and I'll have a black horse—no, it shall be a gray one—and I'll ride up and down the street all day long. Oh how I wish I were a man now!

Soliloquy of the Idle Boy become a Man.

5. Yes, I am a man; and woe is me for having been such a little fool when I was a boy! I hated my book, and took more pains to forget my lessons than ever I did to learn them. What a dunce I

was, even over my spelling! Always at the bottom of my class, and my book thumbed and soiled with dog's-ears and with nail-marks!

6. "Do, Charles, learn your lessons," said my father, "or you will be fit for nothing when a man." "Do, dear Charles, give your mind to your books, or I shall be ashamed of owning you for my boy," said my poor mother. But, no; I must give my mind only to playing marbles, whipping tops, joking with the hostlers, stoning the cats, robbing apple trees and eating cakes; and a fine scholar these things made of me!

7. Now, there was Charles Knight: he liked play well enough, and could skate better, swim farther and jump higher than ever I could; but he liked reading better still; and he learnt more, out of school hours, than ever I did in them. He is now, like myself, a man, but a very different kind of man from me. He has made friends among the wise, the honorable and the learned; I can not be admitted to their acquaintance.

8. He can interest a whole company with useful information; I am obliged either to be silent, or to talk about the weather, or about fast horses. I can tell you about the last great race, but I can not write a letter which is not full of blunders. I see my folly now, but too late. I have no time to read, for I must work for my daily bread; and, if I had time, I could not now turn my reading to profit. Behold the bitter fruits of idleness in childhood!

LESSON XXXV.

BALM'Y (bäm'y), like balm; soothing; fragrant.
COM'PASS-ES (kum'-), encircles.
CON'SE-CRATE, to make sacred.
GAR'NERED, stored up; gathered.
IN-TER-FUSE', to pour between.
'NEATH, a contraction of *beneath* (*th* vocal as in *thine*).
RE-STRAIN', to withhold.
UN-A-WARES', unexpectedly.

Pronounce *tem'pests*, *troub'led* (trub'bld), *heavens* (hev'vns), *'neath*, *plant* (the *a* as in *care*), *fierce*, *dews*, *natural*, *while.*

THE PLANTING OF THE TREE.

"I said to my little son, who was watching, with tears, a tree he had planted, 'Let it alone: it will grow while you are sleeping!'"

I.

"PLANT it safe, thou little child!
Then cease watching and cease weeping:
Thou hast done thy utmost part;
Leave it with a quiet heart—
It will grow while thou art sleeping."

II.

"But oh, father!" said the child,
With a troubled face, close creeping,
"How can I but think and grieve,
When the fierce winds come at eve,
And snows beat, and I lie sleeping?"

III.

Sternly said the father, then:
"Who art thou, child, vainly grieving?
Canst *thou* send the balmy dews,
Or the rich sap interfuse,
That one leaf shall burst to leafing?

IV.

"Canst thou bid the heavens restrain
  Natural tempests for thy praying?
Canst thou bend one tender shoot?
Stay the growth of one frail root?
  Keep one blossom from decaying?

V.

"Plant it; consecrate with prayers:
  It is safe 'neath His sky's folding
Who the whole earth compasses,
Whether we watch more or less—
  His large eye all things beholding."

VI.

If his hope, tear-sown, that child
  Garnered safe with joyful reaping,
Know I not; yet, unawares,
Oft this truth gleams through my prayers,
  "It will grow while thou art sleeping!"

LESSON XXXVI.

A-BID'ING, lasting; permanent.
AL'LEYS, narrow walks.
BED'RID-DEN, confined to bed.
DES'TINED, doomed; appointed.
GEN-ER-A'TIONS, races; families.
IN-HALE', to draw into the lungs as air; to inspire.
PER'ISH-A-BLE, liable to perish.
PROP'ER-TY, possession; quality; that which is one's own.

RICHES WITHOUT WINGS.

1. BY the side of the old bridge yonder stands a tree which I call *mine*. Other generations before me have dwelt under its shade, and called it *theirs*, and other generations after me will do the same. And yet I call the tree *mine*. A bird has

built a nest on one of its highest branches, but I can not reach it, and yet I call the tree *mine.*

2. Mine? There is scarcely any thing which I can call mine, which will not last much longer in this world than I shall. There is not a single button of my coat that is not destined to outlast me many years. I remember an old wood near to the house in which I was born, and not far from

that old bridge which you see. What days have I passed under the thick shade of that wood, and in its green alleys!

3. What violets have I gathered in it in the month of April, and what lilies of the valley in the month of May! What strawberries, blackberries and nuts I have eaten in it! What butterflies I have chased there! What nests I have

discovered! What sweet perfumes have I inhaled! What verses have I made there!

4. How often have I gone thither, at the close of day, to see the glorious sun set, coloring with red and gold the white trunks of the birch trees around me! This wood, my lad, was not *mine;* it belonged to an old, bed-ridden miser, who had, perhaps, never been in it in his life—and yet it *belonged* to him.

5. What, then, can I truly call mine—mine by the grace of our heavenly Father, since all good gifts must come first from *him?* The stores of learning which I lay up in my mind; the virtues with which I adorn my character; the good deeds which I perform; my kindnesses to others, my charities, my fidelity to the right,—these are a kind of property which I shall never lose.

6. I shall take them with me to the higher life which succeeds this life of the body; and they will there be to me one of the sources of my happiness and my joy. Then, my dear boy, let us not be too fond of wealth and the perishable things of this life. Let us rather be fond of those abiding things which we can more truly call *ours;* of the riches that do not make themselves wings and fly away.

"Seek Truth, that pure celestial Truth whose birth
Was in the heaven of heavens; clear, sacred, shrined
In Reason's light: not oft she visits earth,
But her majestic form the willing mind
Through faith may sometimes see. Give her thy soul,
Nor faint, though error's surges 'gainst thee roll."

LESSON XXXVII.

CON-CEIVED′, thought.
CRAFT (kräft), skill; art; trade.
CRAV′ING, begging; desiring.
FAIN (*adv.*), gladly; with joy.
RE-TORT′, a censure returned.
SEC′RE-TA-RY, clerk; scribe.

THE RETORT.

I.

ONE day, a rich man, flushed with pride and wine—
  Sitting with guests at table, all quite merry—
Conceived it would be vastly fine
  To crack a joke upon his secretary.
"Young man," said he, "by what art, craft or trade
  Did your good father earn his livelihood?"
"He was a saddler, sir," the young man said,
  "And in his line was always reckoned good."

II.

"A saddler, eh? and had you stuffed with Greek,
  Instead of teaching you like *him* to do!
And pray, sir, why did not your father make
  A saddler, too, of you?"
At this each flatterer, as in duty bound,
The joke applauded—and the laugh went round.

III.

At length the secretary, bowing low,
  Said (craving pardon if too free he made),
"Sir, by your leave, I fain would know
  Your father's trade?"
"*My* father's *trade?* Why, sir, but that's too bad;
My father's trade! Why, blockhead, art thou mad?
My father, sir, was never brought so low:
He was a gentleman, I'd have you know."

IV.

"Indeed! excuse the liberty I take;
But, if your story's true,
How happened it your father did not make
A gentleman of you?"

LESSON XXXVIII.

AP-POINT'ED, fixed; set.
CHAT'HAM, LORD, a famous English statesman and orator, born 1708, died 1778.
CON-DU'CIVE, leading to; aiding.
CON-TRIB'UTE, to give to; to help.
DIS-PATCH' or DE-SPATCH', speed haste; a message quickly sent.
FOR'TI-FY, to strengthen.
FRIV'O-LOUS, slight; trifling.
LON-GEV'I-TY (-jev'-), long life.
PROG'RESS, motion forward.

EARLY RISING.

1. FEW things contribute so much to preserve health and prolong life as going to bed early and rising early. We lose vigor by lying abed when in health longer than for necessary sleep;

the head is less tranquil; the body is less disposed for refreshing slumber; appetite and digestion are lessened.

2. Old people, examined as to the cause of longevity, all agree that they have been in the habit of going to bed early and rising early. George the Third consulted his physicians, separately, as to the modes of life conducive to health, and they all agreed as to the importance of early rising.

3. The difference of rising every morning at six and eight in the course of forty years amounts to upward of twenty-nine thousand hours, or three years, one hundred and twenty-six days, six hours, so that it is just the same as if ten years of life were to be added, of which we might command eight hours every day for the cultivation of our minds or the dispatch of business.

4. Lord Chatham urged it on his son to rise early. "I never thought," says Daniel Webster, "that Adam had much the advantage of us from having seen the world while it was new. The manifestations of the power of God, like his mercies, are 'new every morning' and fresh every moment. We see as fine risings of the sun as ever Adam saw, and its risings are as much a miracle now as they were in his day, and I think a good deal more. It is now a part of the miracle that for ages the sun has come to his appointed time without the variation of the millionth part of a second."

5. I know a family in which there are three

young sisters who took nearly the whole care of their father's farm when he was absent in Europe some years ago. They would rise early, and while one of them milked the cow, the others would be weeding or hoeing the soil in the garden.

6. These girls then formed habits which have strengthened their constitutions, and have made it easy for them to take a proper amount of exercise out of doors. They love to see the sun rise, and to get through the better part of their household work in good season. Thus they find ample leisure for walking, for reading and for study, at the same time that they fortify and improve their health.

LESSON XXXIX.

A-CHIEVED′, performed.
CEN′TER or CEN′TRE, the middle.
CIR′CU-LAR, round like a circle.
EVEN (e′vn), the evening.
OR′BIT, circular path.
PIS′TON, a cylinder which works up and down in a pump, etc.
PON′DER-OUS, heavy.
PRO-DIG′IOUS (pro-dij′us), wonderful.
STA′TION-A-RY, fixed.
VE-LOC′I-TY (-los′-), swiftness.
VIS′TAS, views; prospects.
VOY′AGE, a passage by sea.
WHER-E′ER′, contraction of *wherever*.

THE EARTH'S JOURNEY ROUND THE SUN.

1. ONE, two, three, four, five! Does the reader know that while he has been counting these five beats, five seconds, he has actually been conveyed through space a distance of more than a hundred miles? Yet so it is. However incredible it may seem, no fact is more certain than that the earth is constantly on the wing, flying around the sun with

a velocity so prodigious that for every breath we draw we advance on our way forty or fifty miles.

2. If, when passing across the waters in a steam-boat, we can awake after a night's repose and find ourselves conducted on our voyage a hundred miles, we exult in the triumph of art which has moved so ponderous a body as a steam-ship over such a space in so short a time, and so quietly, too, as not to disturb our slumbers; but, with a motion vastly more quiet and uniform, we have, in the same interval, been carried along with the earth in its orbit more than half a million of miles.

3. In the case of the steam-ship, however perfect the machinery may be, we still, in our waking hours at least, are made sensible of the action of the forces by which the motion is maintained, as the roaring of the fire, the beating of the piston and the dashing of the paddle-wheels; but in the more perfect machinery which carries the earth forward on its grander voyage, no sound is heard, nor the least intimation afforded of the stupendous forces by which this motion is achieved.

4. The distance of the sun from the earth is about ninety-five millions of miles. No human mind can comprehend fully what this vast distance means. But we may form some conception of it by such an illustration as this: A ship may leave Liverpool and cross the Atlantic to New York after twenty days' steady sail, but it would take that ship, moving at the rate of ten miles an hour, more than a thousand years to reach the sun.

5. And yet, at this vast distance, the sun, by his power of attraction, serves as the great regulatoı of the planetary motions, bending them continually from the straight line in which they tend to move, and compelling them to circulate around him, each at nearly a uniform distance, and all in perfect harmony. Consider the wonderful force which the sun must put forth to bend out of their courses into circular orbits such a number of planets, some of them more than a thousand times larger than the earth!

6. Were a ship-of-war under full sail, we can easily imagine what a force it would require to turn her from her course by a rope attached to her bow, especially were it required that the force should remain stationary, and the ship be so held as to be made to go round the force as round a center. Somewhat similar to this, but on a much grander scale, is the action which is exerted on the earth in its journey round the sun.

7. By an invisible influence which we call *gravitation* the sun turns all the planets out of their course, and bends them into a circular orbit round himself, though they are all many millions of times more ponderous than the ship, and are moving many thousand times more swiftly.

8. The heavenly bodies appear small to the eye of an inhabitant of this earth only from the immensity of their distance. When we talk of hundreds of millions of miles, it is not to be listened to as incredible. For remember that we are talk-

ing of those bodies which are scattered over the immensity of space, and that space knows no termination. The conception is great and difficult, but the truth is unquestionable.

THOU ART, O GOD.

I.

Thou art, O God, the life and light
  Of all this wondrous world we see;
Its glow by day, its smile by night,
  Are but reflections caught from thee:
Where'er we turn thy glories shine,
And all things fair and bright are thine!

II.

When day, with farewell beam, delays
  Among the opening clouds of even,
And we can almost think we gaze
  Through golden vistas into heaven,
Those hues that mark the sun's decline,
So soft, so radiant, Lord, are thine.

III.

When night, with wings of starry gloom,
  O'ershadows all the earth and skies,
Like some dark, beauteous bird, whose plume
  Is sparkling with a thousand eyes,
That sacred gloom, those fires divine,
So grand, so countless, Lord, are thine.

IV.

When youthful spring around us breathes,
  Thy spirit warms her fragrant sigh;
And every flower the summer wreathes
  Is born beneath that kindling eye:
Where'er we turn thy glories shine,
And all things fair and bright are thine!

LESSON XL.

THE PHILOSOPHER AND THE BOATMAN.

Philosopher. Boatman, I am afraid you do not know as much as a man of your years ought to know. For instance, What do you know of algebra?

Boatman. Algebra, sir? I never heard of it before. I know nothing about it.

Phil. Then a quarter of your life is lost. But perhaps you know something of metaphysics?

Boatman. Met a what, sir? Ah, you mean to ask if I ever took physic! Not much, sir. Physic isn't in my line.

Phil. Excuse me. I asked if you knew anything of metaphysics, the science which relates to the ultimate grounds of being, as distinguished from its phenomenal modifications.

Boatman. I never heard the word before, sir; my father was a fisherman, and he took me to sea with him as soon as I was strong enough to pull a brickbat in at the chamber window. I know nothing of meta—what do you call it?

Phil. If you know nothing of metaphysics, boatman, you have lost another quarter of your life.

Boatman. That's a hard case, isn't it? Two quarters make a half.

Phil. But perhaps you know something of astronomy, boatman?

Boatman. Not a bit of it, sir—not a bit of it! I've had other things to attend to.

Phil. Then you have lost another quarter of your— Eh? What's the matter with the boat? Is it sinking? What are you pulling off your coat for?

Boatman. Don't you see that the boat has sprung a leak, and is sinking?

Phil. Sinking? Eh? What do you mean?

Boatman. You'll find out pretty soon. Can you swim?

Phil. Swim? Of course I can't swim. You don't expect a philosopher like me to swim, do you?

Boatman. Then if you can't swim, the *whole* of *your* life is lost; for the boat is going to the bottom, and no mistake.

LESSON XLI.

AP-PRO′PRI-ATE, *a.*, fit; proper.

AR′BI-TRA-RY, *a.*, absolute; governed by will only.

CLAUSE (klauz), *n.*, separate member of a sentence.

COUP′LET (kŭp′let), *n.*, two verses.

DIS-PERSE′, *v. t.*, to scatter; to dispel.

IN-VIS′I-BLE, *a.*, not to be seen.

PEERAGE, *n.*, the class of peers.

PER-FECT′ED, finished.

PROM′I-NENT, *a.*, standing out.

SO-LIC′I-TOUS (-lis′-), anxious.

SPEC′IAL (spĕsh′al), *a.*, designed for a particular purpose.

STRESS, *n.*, force; weight.

TRAG′E-DY (traj′e-dy), *n.*, a dramatic poem; a fatal event.

Pronounce *Mirabeau, Mir′a-bo; pronunciation, pro-nun-she-a′-shun.* Do not say *empasis* for *em′pha-sis* (*em′fa-sis*); *spiled* for *spoiled. Re′al-ly* is in three syllables. Do not call it *reely.* In *cer′tain, cap′tain, moun′tain*, etc., *ai* has the sound of short ĭ.

HOW TO READ WELL.

1. PRONUNCIATION is the utterance of words with those vowel and consonant sounds, and that accent, which the best usage has established. Thus, pronunciation teaches us to say *ve′he-ment* instead of *ve-he′-ment; mis′chiev-ous* instead of *mis-chiev′ous;* and to sound the *ou* in *group* and *soup* like *o* in *move*, instead of like *ou* in *house.* The correct pronunciation of words can be best learnt by consulting the dictionary.

2. Pronunciation properly includes articulation "In just articulation," says Austin, "the words are not hurried over, nor precipitated syllable over syllable. They are delivered out from the lips, as beautiful coins, newly issued from the mint, deeply and accurately impressed, perfectly finished, neatly struck by the proper organs; distinct, sharp, in due succession, and of due weight."

3. Inflections of the voice are those upward and downward slides in tone by which we express either the suspension or the completion of the meaning of what we utter, as in the following sentence: "As trees and plants come from seeds, so are you, An'tony, the seed of this most calamitous war." Here the voice slides up at the end of the first clause, at *seeds*, as the sense is not perfected, and slides down at the completion of the sense, at the word *war*, where the sentence ends.

4. Emphasis is that peculiar stress which we lay upon particular words to bring out their meaning or importance more directly. Thus, in the following couplet from Pope, there is an example of emphasis:

> "'Tis hard to say if greater want of skill
> Appear in writing or in judging ill."

Here the words *writing* and *judging* are opposed to each other, and are, therefore, the emphatical words. In the following couplet, by Cowper, if you properly study the sense, you cannot well go astray in laying the proper stress on the proper words:

> "A modest, sensible and well-bred man
> Would not insult me, and no other can."

5. Arbitrary rules are of little value in teaching to read. If you fully understand and feel what you are reading, if you can pronounce all the words correctly, and if you have acquired facility

of utterance by practice, you will be likely to read aright. "Probably not a single instance," says Archbishop Whately, "could be found, of any one who has attained, by the study of any system of instruction, a really good delivery; but there are many—probably nearly as many as have fully tried the experiment—who have by this means been totally spoiled."

6. In familiar discourse we rarely fail to place the emphasis properly; and this is because we fully understand what we are saying. In order, therefore, to give the right emphasis to what we read aloud, we should acquaint ourselves with the meaning and construction of every sentence; for emphasis is, as it were, the invisible *gesticulation* of the mind through the voice, and all rules must give way to it.

7. Dispose the emphasis aright in the following sentence: "The pleasures of the imagination are not so gross as those of sense, nor so refined as those of the understanding." In this example, the emphatic words, *gross* and *refined*, are opposed to each other, and contrasted with *sense* and *understanding*

"He raised a mortal to the skies;
She drew an angel down."

Here three emphatic words in the first line are opposed to three in the second.

8. In the following passage, from Addison's tragedy of "Cato," the italicized words ought to be the most emphatic; and the parenthetical clause

ought to be spoken in a lower tone of voice, and with a more rapid utterance, than the principal sentence; a slight pause, both before and after the parenthesis, being appropriate.

> "If there's a Power above us
> (And that there *is*, all Nature cries aloud
> Through all her works), he must delight in *virtue;*
> And that which *he* delights in must be happy."

9. The reply of Mirabeau to the messenger of the king, who had ordered the French National Assembly to disperse, presents two emphatic words, which the reader who comprehends and feels the speech will not be slow to detect: "Go say to those who sent you that we are here by the power of the people, and that we will not be driven hence save by the power of the bayonet."

10. The following passage, in the reply of Lord Thurlow to the Duke of Grafton, contains at least eight prominently emphatic words: "No one venerates the Peerage more than *I* do; but, my lords, I must say that the Peerage solicited *me*—not *I* the Peerage. Nay, more—I can say, and *will* say, that, as a peer of Parliament, as Speaker of this right honorable house, as keeper of the great seal, as guardian of his majesty's conscience, as Lord High Chancellor of England—nay, even in that character alone in which the noble duke would think it an affront to be considered, but which character none can deny *me*—as a *man*—I am, at this moment, as *respectable*—I beg leave to add, as

much *respected*—as the proudest peer I now look down upon."

11. Few positive rules for reading can be laid down to which many unforeseen exceptions cannot be taken. Give the *sense* of what you read. *Mind* is the thing. Pauses are essential only where the omission would obscure the sense. The orator who, in the act of delivery, is studiously solicitous about parceling his words, is sure to leave the best part of his work undone. He delivers words, not thoughts. Deliver thoughts, and words will take care enough of themselves, providing always that you have acquired the proper accuracy in pronunciation.

LESSON XLII.

AD-HER′ING (-hēre′-), sticking fast.
AN′NU-AL, yearly.
EX-PAN′SION, spreading; opening.
GATH′ER-ING (găth′-), collecting.
HERB (erb or herb), a plant that dies to the root every year.
MOLD′Y or MOULD′Y, filled with mold.
PER-EN′NI-AL, lasting; constant.
PROC′ESS (prŏs′es), course; progress; mode of operation.
PROD′UCE, yield; product.
STA′PLE, the thread or fiber of wool, cotton or flax; chief commodity.
TRI-AN′GU-LAR (-ăng′-), having three angles.

THE COTTON PLANT.

1. OF the four raw materials which supply clothing, *flax* is said to have belonged originally to Egypt; the sheep, which furnishes *wool*, to the mountain ranges of Asia; the *silk*-worm to China, and the *cotton* plant to India and America.

2. Although cotton was not generally known among the nations of the earth until at a much later period than the other substances, it is now raised in such abundance as to be the cheapest of all clothing. From its great resemblance to sheep's wool, it was called by the ancients "the wool of trees," and although it differs greatly from the animal fleece, the term is still retained. The Germans call it tree-wool, and the French give it a name which answers to the English term cotton wool.

3. The many varieties of the cotton-plant have been divided into *herb*-cotton, *shrub*-cotton and *tree*-cotton, according to the mode of growth. Of these the most useful is the herb-cotton, which is extensively cultivated in the southern parts of the United States of America, in India, China and other warm climates.

4. The most esteemed variety of the herb-cotton is that known by the name of *sea-island* cotton, which is of *long staple*, its fiber being much longer than that of any other description, and of a fine silky texture. It is an annual plant, and being found to thrive in the low sandy islands which lie along the coast from Charleston to Savannah, the cotton hence derives its name.

5. Herb-cotton attains a height of from eighteen to twenty-four inches. Its leaves are of a dark green color. The blossom expands into a pale yellow flower, which falling off, a pointed triangular pod appears. This gradually increases to the

size of a large filbert, and becomes brown as the woolly fruit ripens.

6. The expansion of the wool then causes the pod to burst, when there appears a ball of snowy white or yellowish down adhering to the seeds. The appearance of a cotton-field while the pods are opening is highly interesting, the fine dark green of the leaf contrasting beautifully with the brilliant white of the cotton suspended from the pods, and floating to and fro at the bidding of the wind.

7. Shrub-cotton grows in most countries where the annual herb-cotton is found. In the West Indies its duration is about two or three years; in India, Egypt and some other places it lasts from six to ten years. In the hottest countries it is perennial, and furnishes two crops a year. In cooler climates it is an annual plant. In appearance it is much like a currant bush.

8. Tree-cotton grows in India, China, Egypt, and in the interior and on the western coast of Africa, and in some parts of America. It attains a height of from twelve to twenty feet.

9. Great care is bestowed in America upon the cultivation of the cotton plant. The seed is sown by hand in March, April or May, according to the season. It is planted in rows five feet asunder, and in holes eighteen inches apart, in each of which several seeds are placed. As the plants come up, the weakest are drawn out, only two or three being left in each hole.

10. Good cotton cannot be produced without

constant care and attention up to the time of flowering. In India, the mode of cultivation is very slovenly, and little or no care is bestowed on the plant; the consequence of which is that the produce is greatly inferior to that of the United States.

11. The operation of gathering the cotton requires much care. The usual method is to take away the seeds and cotton, leaving the empty husks. The gathering is always performed in fine weather, after the morning dew has disappeared, as any moisture would make the cotton moldy, and cause the oil of the seed to spread over the wool. The cotton is more completely dried by exposure during several days to the heat of the sun or of stoves, whereby the seeds are afterward more easily separated.

12. As the cotton does not all ripen at the same time, the gatherers have to go over the same plantation many times. If it is not gathered soon after the pods have burst, the heat of the sun injures its color, or it may be blown away by the wind or spoiled by the rain or dew. More than four-fifths of the cotton at present used in Great Britain is from the United States, where the cotton now produced exceeds the production of the whole world in 1770; and this is to be attributed in some degree to the good quality of American cotton, the low price of land, and the improvements introduced into the various processes of planting, cleaning and packing.

LESSON XLIII.

BIRD′LING, a little bird.
EX-ULT′ING (ĕgz-), rejoicing.
RE-SPOND′, to answer; to reply.
TEEM′ING, abounding; full.

PLEASANT WEATHER.

I.

THANK God for pleasant weather! Chant it, merry rills,
And clap your hands together, ye exulting hills!
Thank him, teeming valley, thank him, fruitful plain,
For the golden sunshine and the silver rain.

II.

Thank God, of good the Giver; shout it, sportive breeze,
Respond, O tuneful river, to the nodding trees;

Thank him, bird and birdling, as ye grow and sing;
Mingle in thanksgiving, every living thing!

III.

Thank God with cheerful spirit, in a glow of love,
For what we here inherit, and our hopes above.
Universal nature revels in her birth
When God, in pleasant weather, smiles upon the earth.

LESSON XLIV.

BAL′LAD, a short narrative song.
DE-TER′, to restrain by fear.
DIC′TION, language; style.
FOOLS′CAP, a kind of writing paper.
MAIN-TAIN′, to assert; to uphold.
ME′TER, or ME′TRE, measure as applied to verse.
PED′ANT, one who makes a vain parade of his knowledge.
PHRASE, a form of speech.
PLA′GI-A-RIST (-je-), one who passes off another's writings as his own.
SON′NET, a poem of fourteen lines.

THE QUARREL OF THE AUTHORS.

Enter BAVIUS *and* MEVIUS, *meeting.*

Bavius. Sir, I'm proud to have met you. Long have I known
Your productions—how often I've wished them my own!
Your verses have charms nowhere else to be found.

Mevius. In *yours* all the graces of diction abound.

Ba. Your phrases are neat, your style charmingly light.

Me. There are touches of nature in all that you write.

Ba. Your odes, how delightful! how tender and true!
What dunce would compare Pope or Pindar to you?
Me. Your songs have a noble and elegant vein
That even old Horace could never attain.
Ba. Can any thing equal your love-ditties rare?
Me. Can aught with your wonderful sonnets compare?
Ba. If the public could estimate half of your worth—
Me. If merit now met its due honors on earth—
Ba. You'd roll thro' the streets in a carriage of gold.
Me. Every square in the city your statue would hold.
Now, this ballad of mine—your opinion upon it,
I should like to—
Ba. Pray, sir, have you met with a sonnet
On the flag of our country?
Me. A sonnet? Just so.
'Twas read at a party, a few nights ago.
Ba. Do you know who's the author?
Me. I know not—nor care;
For 'tis an exceedingly trifling affair.
Ba. Yet many admire it—or so they tell *me.*
Me. No matter for that; it's as bad as can be.
And could you but read it, sir, you'd say so too.
Ba. But—but, sir, I'm sorry to differ from you;
Every person of taste its merit must strike.
Me. May the Muses deter me from making the like!

Ba. I maintain that a better the world cannot show;
For I am the author—yes, *I*, you must know.
Me. You?
Ba. I, I, sir, I, I!
Me. Well, I wonder indeed how that came to pass.
Ba. I had the ill-luck not to please you, alas!
Me. Perhaps there was something distracted my head;
Or else the man spoiled it, so badly he read.
But here is my ballad, concerning which I—
Ba. Oh, out upon ballads! their day is gone by;
The ballad is obsolete—out of date quite.
Me. Yet, even now, many in ballads delight.
Ba. What of that, sir? I think them decidedly flat.
Me. *You* think them! Perhaps they're no worse, sir, for that.
Ba. For pedants, indeed, they have charms beyond measure.
Me. Then how can it be they afford *you* no pleasure?
Ba. You give others qualities found but in *you*.
Me. You call others names that are justly *your* due.
Go, blotter of foolscap! contemptible creature!
Ba. Go, scribbler of sonnets, and butcher of meter!
Me. Go, impudent plagiarist! Blockhead, get out!

Ba. Go, rascal! Be careful! mind what you're about!

Me. Go, go! strip your writings of each borrowed plume;
Let the Greeks and the Latins your plunder resume.

Ba. Go, you, and ask pardon of Venus and Bacchus,
For your lame imitations of witty old Flaccus.*

Me. Remember your book's insignificant sale.

Ba. Remember your bookseller driven to jail.

Me. My pen shall avenge me—to your great disaster!

Ba. And mine shall inform you, sir, who is your master.

Me. I defy you in verse, English, Latin or Greek!

Ba. You shall hear from me, sir, in the course of the week.

NOW IS THE TIME.

THE bud will soon become a flower, the flower become a seed;
Then seize, O youth! the present hour—of that thou hast most need.
Do thy best always—do it *now*—for, in the present time,
As in the furrows of a plow, fall seeds of good or crime.

---

* Quintus Horatius Flaccus, or Horace, a famous Roman poet, born 65 B.C. Venus was the goddess of love, and Bacchus the god of wine, in the ancient mythology.

The sun and rain will ripen fast each seed that thou hast sown,
And every act and word at last by its own fruit be known;
And soon the harvest of thy toil rejoicing thou shalt reap,
Or, o'er thy wild, neglected soil, go forth in shame to weep.

LESSON XLV.

AB'SO-LUTE, complete; certain.
AD'VER-SA-RY, an enemy.
CON-GE'NI-AL, of the same nature.
DIS'SO-LUTE, loose; depraved.
FEL'ON, one guilty of a capital crime.
FUL'MI-NATE, to thunder.
GLAD'I-A-TOR, a sword-player.
HORDE, a wandering band.
MIS'CRE-ANT, a vile wretch.
RAP'ĬNE, act of plundering.
SCHEME (skēme), a plot; a plan.
TRAI'TOR, one who betrays trust.
TREACH'ER-Y, breach of faith.

CICERO AGAINST CATILINE.

1. AT length, Romans, we are rid of Catiline! We have driven him forth, drunk with fury, fulminating mischief, threatening to revisit us with fire and sword. He has gone; he has fled; he has escaped; he has broken away. No longer within the very walls of the city shall he plot her ruin.

2. We have forced him from secret schemes into open rebellion. The bad citizen is now the avowed traitor. His flight is the confession of his treason. Would that his attendants had not been so few! Be speedy, ye companions of his dissolute pleasures—be speedy, and you may overtake him, before night, on the Aurelian road.

3. Let him not languish, deprived of your society. Haste to rejoin the congenial crew that

compose his army—*his* army, I say; for who can doubt that the army under Manlius expect Catiline for their leader? And such an army! Outcasts from honor, and fugitives from debt; gamblers and felons; miscreants, whose dreams are of rapine, murder and conflagration!

4. Against these desperate troops of your adversary prepare, O Romans! your garrisons and armies. And first, to that maimed and battered gladiator oppose your consuls and generals. Next, against that miserable outcast horde lead forth the strength and flower of all Italy!

5. On the one side chastity contends; on the other, wantonness; here purity, there pollution; here integrity, there treachery; here piety, there profanity; here constancy, there rage; here honesty, there baseness; here continence, there lust.

6. In short, equity, temperance, fortitude, prudence, struggle with iniquity, luxury, cowardice, rashness—every virtue with every vice! And, lastly, the contest lies between well-grounded hope and absolute despair. In such a conflict, were every human aid to fail, would not Providence empower such conspicuous virtue to triumph over such complicated vice?

IMMORTALITY OF TRUTH.

TRUTH, crushed to earth, shall rise again;
The eternal years of God are hers;
But Error, wounded, writhes with pain,
And dies among her worshipers.—BRYANT.

LESSON XLVI.

AT′TRI-BUTES, qualities; properties.
CON-SUM′MATE, complete; perfect.
DE-FENSE′ or DE-FENCE′, protection.
PA′TRI-OT, lover of one's country.
PA′TRON, defender; protector.
RE-LIN′QUISH-MENT (-lĭng′-), an abandonment.
SAN′GUINE (săng′gwin), ardent.
SCAB′BARD (skab′-), sheath; case.
SU-PREME′, highest in power.

CHARACTER OF WASHINGTON.

1. THIS eminent person is presented to our observation clothed in attributes as modest, as unpretending, as little calculated to strike or to astonish, as if he had passed unknown through some secluded region of private life. But he had a judgment sure and sound; a steadiness of mind which never suffered any passion, or even any feeling, to ruffle its calm; a strength of under-

standing which worked rather than forced its way through all obstacles, removing or avoiding rather than overleaping them.

2. This is the consummate glory of Washington: he was a triumphant warrior where the most sanguine had a right to despair; a successful ruler in all the difficulties of a course wholly untried; but a warrior whose sword only left its sheath when the first law of our nature commanded it to be drawn, and a ruler who, having tasted of supreme power, gently and unostentatiously desired that the cup might pass from him, nor would suffer more to wet his lips than the most solemn and sacred duty to his country and his God required.

3. To his latest breath did this great patriot maintain the noble character of a captain the patron of peace and a statesman the friend of justice. Dying, he bequeathed to his heirs the sword which he had worn in the war for liberty, and charged them "never to take it from the scabbard but in self-defense, or in the defense of their country and her freedom," and commanded them that, "when it should thus be drawn, they should never sheathe it, nor ever give it up, but prefer falling with it in their hands to the relinquishment thereof"—words the majesty and simple eloquence of which are not surpassed in the oratory of Athens and Rome.

4. It will be the duty of the historian and the sage, in all ages, to let no occasion pass of commemorating this illustrious man, and until time

shall be no more will a test of the progress which our race has made in wisdom and in virtue be derived from the veneration paid to the immortal name of WASHINGTON!

LESSON XLVII.

E-THE′RE-AL, airy; celestial.

FIRM′A-MENT, sky; the heavens.

GAL-I-LE′O, a great astronomer and philosopher, was born at Pisa (pronounced *Pee′za*), in Tuscany, 1564, died 1642.

IM-PER-CEP′TI-BLE, not to be seen.

IN-DI-VID′U-AL, single; one.

IN′FLU-ENCE, power of directing.

IN′TER-VAL, space between.

IN-VES′TI-GATE, to examine.

MUT′U-AL (mūt′yu-al), interchanged; common.

NEWTON, SIR ISAAC, born in England 1642, died 1727.

O-RIG′I-NAL (rij′-), source; cause.

RE′AL, actual; true; genuine.

TER-RES′TRI-AL, earthly; worldly.

THERE′FORE (thêr′for), for that.

TO′WARD (tō′ard), in the direction of; with direction to.

U-NI-VERS′AL, total; whole.

WHAT IS GRAVITATION?

1. WE discover in nature a tendency of every portion of matter toward every other. This tendency is called the *law of gravitation.* In obedience to this power, a stone falls to the ground and a planet revolves around the sun. The former is an example of what we call *gravity;* the latter an example of universal *gravitation.*

2. The laws of terrestrial gravity were first investigated by Galileo, those of universal gravitation by Sir Isaac Newton. Terrestrial gravity is only an individual example of universal gravitation, being the tendency of bodies toward the center of the earth. We are so much accustomed, from

our earliest years, to see bodies fall to the earth, that we imagine they must of necessity fall "downward;" but when we reflect that the earth is round, and that bodies fall toward the center on all sides of it—and that, of course, on opposite sides of the earth they fall in precisely opposite directions and toward each other—we perceive that there must be some force acting to produce this effect.

3. Every motion implies some force which produces it, and the fact that bodies fall toward the earth on all sides of it leads us to infer that that force, whatever it is, resides in the earth itself. We therefore call it *attraction.* We do not, however, say what attraction *is*, but what it *does.*

4. We must bear in mind, also, that this attraction is mutual—that when a stone falls toward the earth, it exerts the same force on the earth that the earth exerts on the stone; but the motion of the earth toward the stone is as much less than that of the stone toward the earth as its quantity of matter is greater, and therefore its motion is quite imperceptible.

5. But although we are compelled to acknowledge the *existence* of such a force as gravity, causing a tendency in all bodies toward each other, yet we know nothing of its *nature*, nor can we conceive by what medium bodies at such a distance as the sun and the earth exercise this influence on each other. Still, we know that it is this which, acting across an interval of ninety-five millions of miles, holds the earth as surely in its orbit as if it were

connected by a chain to the sun, and the same force holds all the other planets in *their* orbits.

6. It is a law of nature that a body when at rest remains so, unless some force puts it in motion, but when once in motion it will continue to move for ever, unless something stops it. When a ball is rolled on the ground, the friction of the earth and the resistance of the air soon stop its motion; when rolled on smooth ice it will go much farther, because the ice opposes much less resistance than the ground, and were there no impediment to its motion, it would continue to move for ever.

7. The earth, and all the other planets which revolve around the sun as their common center, are actually in this condition. They would fly off into space, and continue to move for ever in a straight line; but, held in check, in obedience to the laws of Him who created them and gave them motion, they circulate in their appointed orbits.

"The spacious firmament on high,
With all the blue ethereal sky,
And spangled heavens, a shining frame,
Their great Original proclaim.
The unwearied sun, from day to day,
Does his Creator's power display,
And publishes to every land
The work of an almighty Hand.

"Soon as the evening shades prevail,
The moon takes up the wondrous tale,
And nightly to the listening earth
Repeats the story of her birth;
While all the stars that round her burn,
And all the planets in their turn,

Confirm the tidings as they roll,
And spread the truth from pole to pole.

"What though in solemn silence all
Move round the dark terrestrial ball?
What though no real voice, nor sound,
Amid their radiant orbs be found?
In reason's ear they all rejoice,
And utter forth a glorious voice;
For ever singing, as they shine,
'The Hand that made us is divine.'"

ADDISON.

JOSEPH ADDISON, the author of the foregoing verses, was born in England in 1672 and died in 1719. Of the verses themselves the late Mr. Thackeray remarks: "Who can listen to their sacred music without love and awe? When this man looks up to the heaven which shines over us all, I can hardly fancy a human face lighted up with a more serene rapture, a human intellect thrilling with a purer love and adoration, than Joseph Addison's.

"It seems to me that those verses shine like the stars. They shine out of a great deep calm. When he turns to heaven, a Sabbath comes over that man's mind, and his face lights up from it with a glory of thanks and prayer. His sense of religion stirs through his whole being. His was a life prosperous and beautiful, a calm death, an immense fame, and affection afterward for his happy and spotless name."

LESSON XLVIII.

BRU′IN, a name given to the bear (from the French *brun*, brown.)

COU′GAR (koo′gar), a panther.

CRIT′I-CIS-ING (-sīz-), judging as a critic.

CROUCH (krowch), to bend low.

EC-CEN′TRIC, irregular; odd.

FEINT (fānt), a mock attack.

GRA-TU′I-TOUS, given without an equivalent.

MAN′DI-BLES (-blz), lower jaws.

MYR′I-AD (mĭr′), ten thousand.

O-RANG′-OU-TANG′ (oo-tăng′), a large monkey.

QUADRILLE (kă-dril′), a dance of sets of dancers, four in a set.

SOM′ER-SET (sŭm′-), a leap in which the heels are thrown over the head.

STREWN (stroon or strōn), scattered loosely.

WRESTLE (rĕs′sl), to strive, as two persons, by trying who shall throw the other down.

FUN AMONG ANIMALS.

1. FUN is not confined to boys and girls. Some of the smallest insects, after their ordinary toils, enjoy themselves in some kind of sport. They

run races, wrestle, and, out of fun, carry each other on their backs much in the same way as boys perform a similar act. A small species of ant, in the intervals of their industry, have been seen doing this, the rider holding with his mandibles on to the neck of his bearer, and embracing it closely with his legs. After being carried a certain length, the rider would be carefully set down.

2. "It is a happy world, after all," says Paley. "The air, the earth, the water, teem with delighted existence. In a spring noon or summer evening on whichever side I turn my eyes, myriads of happy beings crowd upon my view. The insect youth are on the wing. Swarms of new-born flies are trying their pinions in the air. Their sportive motions, their wanton mazes, their gratuitous activity, their continual change of place, without use or purpose, testify their joy and the exultation which they feel in their lately-discovered faculties."

3. Small birds chase each other about in play. The trumpeter-bird hops about in the most eccentric manner on one leg, and throws somersets. The crane expands its wings, runs round in circles, leaps, and throwing little stones and pieces of wood in the air, endeavors to catch them again, or pretends to avoid them, as if afraid. Water-birds, such as ducks and geese, dive after each other, and cleave the surface of the water, with out-stretched neck and flapping wings, throwing an abundant spray around.

4. There is a story told of a tame magpie which was seen busily engaged in a garden gathering pebbles, and, with much solemnity and a studied air, dropping them into a hole about eighteen inches deep, made to receive a post. After dropping each stone it cried "Currack!" triumphantly, and set off for another. On examining the spot, a poor toad was found in the hole, which the magpie was stoning for his amusement.

5. The mocking-bird seems to take delight in imitating the noises made by other animals, and by man himself. It whistles for the dog; Cæsar starts up, wags his tail, and runs to meet his master. It squeaks out like a hurt chicken, and the hen hurries about with hanging wings and bristled feathers, clucking to protect her injured brood. The barking of the dog, the mewing of the cat, the creaking of a passing wheelbarrow, are all imitated by this little creature with surprising truth and rapidity.

6. Deer often engage in a sham battle, or a trial of strength, by twisting their horns together and pushing for the mastery. All animals that pretend violence in their play stop short of exercising it; the dog takes the greatest precaution not to injure by his bite, and the orang-outang, in wrestling with his keeper, pretends to throw him, and makes a feint of biting him.

7. Some animals carry out in their play the semblance of catching their prey: young cats, for instance, leap after every small and moving object,

even to the leaves strewn by the autumn wind; they crouch and steal forward, ready for a spring, the body quivering and the tail vibrating with emotion. They bound on the moving leaf, and again spring forward to another. Young tigers and cougars have been found playing with round substances as kittens do with a ball of yarn.

8. The kitten is familiar to us all as the very embodiment of playfulness. A young friend of mine has a kitten she calls Dot. It would surprise you to see to how many liberties, short of being tied in a bow-knot, Dot will submit. With a doll's cap on her head she cuts a very comical figure. Her mistress rules her by tenderness: she takes care never to hurt her.

9. The California Indians say that the cubs of the bear go through all sorts of queer little antics, very often apparently for the sole purpose of distressing their anxious parents. The grown-up bears engage in dances, and the places where such sports have been held are detected by the Indians from the manner in which the ground is beaten.

10. Sometimes a bear will dance by himself, while others squat down and look on, as if criticising the performance. At other times a whole party of bears will join in a sort of quadrille. The custom proves that Bruin, though his exterior is rough and his ordinary deportment by no means graceful, knows how to relax among his equals, and is not indifferent to social amusement.

LESSON XLIX.

A-CHIEVE'MENT, deed; exploit.
AL'IEN (āle'yen), a foreigner.
BLENCHED, shrank; started back.
CON-FED'ER-ATE, an ally.
IM-POS'TURE, deception; cheat.
IN-FLEX-I-BIL'I-TY, firmness.
LE'GION, a body of soldiers.
PHAL'ANX, a close body of troops.
STARK, *a.*, stiff; *ad.*, wholly.
VO-CAB'U-LA-RY, a list of words.

Pronounce Assaye (in Hin-dos-tan), *As-sī'ye;* Vimieira (in Portugal), *Ve-may'e-rah;* Badajos (in Spain), *Bad-a-hōs;* Albuera (in Spain), *Al-boo-ā'ra;* Toulouse (in France), *Too-looz'.*

The following eloquent remarks were made by Richard Lalor Shiel in the British Parliament in 1837, in reply to Lord Lyndhurst, who had spoken of the Irish as "aliens." Lyndhurst, born in Boston, Mass., 1772, died in England, 1863. Shiel, born in Dublin, Ireland, 1791, died 1851.

SHIEL'S REPLY TO LORD LYNDHURST.

1. I SHOULD be surprised, indeed, if, while you are doing us wrong, you did not profess your solicitude to do us justice. Englishmen were never wanting in such protestations. There is, however, one exception. There is a man of great abilities—not a member of this House, but whose talents and boldness have placed him in the topmost place in his party—who has been heard to speak of the Irish as "aliens." Disdaining all imposture, and abandoning all reserve, he distinctly and audaciously tells the Irish people that they are not entitled to the same privileges as Englishmen, that they are "aliens." Aliens? Good heavens! Was Arthur, Duke of Wellington, in the House of Lords, and did he not start up and exclaim, "Hold! I have seen the aliens do their duty?"

2. The Duke of Wellington is not a man of an

excitable temperament. His mind is of a cast too martial to be easily moved, but notwithstanding his habitual inflexibility, I can not help thinking that when he heard his countrymen designated by a phrase as offensive as the abundant vocabulary of his eloquent confederate could supply,—I can not help thinking that he ought to have recollected the many fields of fight in which we have been contributors to his renown.

3. The "battles, sieges, fortunes, that he has passed," ought to have come back upon him. He ought to have remembered that, from the earliest achievement in which he displayed that military genius which has placed him foremost in the annals of modern warfare, down to that last and surpassing combat which has made his name imperishable—from Assaye to Waterloo—the Irish soldiers, with whom your armies are filled, were the inseparable auxiliaries to the glory with which his unparalleled successes have been crowned.

4. Whose were the arms that drove your bayonets at Vimieira through the phalanxes that never reeled in the shock of war before? What desperate valor climbed the steeps and filled the moats of Badajos? All, all his victories should have rushed and crowded back upon his memory; Vimieira, Badajos, Salamanca, Albuera, Toulouse, and, last of all,* the greatest—

* The tone of suspension should be given at *greatest*, the dash indicating a sudden break in the speaker's remarks. The battle he there refers to is Waterloo, fought against Napoleon, June 18, 1815. The

5. Tell me, for you were there—I appeal to the gallant soldier before me, who bears, I know, a generous heart in an intrepid breast—tell me, for you must needs remember, on that day, when the destinies of mankind were trembling in the balance, while death fell in showers; when the artillery of France, leveled with the precision of the most deadly science, played upon them; when her legions, incited by the voice, inspired by the example, of their mighty leader, rushed again and again to the onset,—tell me if, for an instant, when to hesitate for an instant was to be lost, the "aliens" blenched!

6. And when, at length, the moment for the last decisive movement had arrived; when the valor, so long wisely checked, was at last let loose; when, with words familiar but immortal, the great captain commanded the great assault,—tell me if Catholic Ireland, with less heroic valor than the natives of your own glorious isle, precipitated herself upon the foe! The blood of England, Scotland, Ireland, flowed in the same stream, drenched the same field.

7. When the chill morning dawned, their dead lay cold and stark together. In the same deep pit their bodies were deposited. The green corn of spring is now breaking from their commingled

---

opposing forces were commanded by Wellington, whose "words," to which the orator alludes, were, "Up, Guards, and at them!" Sir Henry Hardinge was the "gallant soldier" to whom personally Shiel appealed in the beautiful transition he made from the simple reference to Waterloo in the one word *greatest*.

dust; the dew falls from heaven upon their union in the grave! Partakers in every peril, in the glory shall we not be permitted to participate? And shall we be told, as a requital, that we are estranged from the noble country for whose salvation our life-blood was poured out?

LESSON L.

AP-PALL′ (-päl′), to terrify; daunt.
A-TONE′, to make amends.
DE-SPOND′, to despair; to give up.
DI-VERT′, to turn aside; to amuse.
PELF, money; gain; wealth.
REC′RE-ANT, cowardly; craven.
SPELL, charm; incantation.
UN-DAUNT′ED (-dänt-), fearless.

UP, FAINT HEART, UP!

I.

UP, faint heart, up! immortal life is lodged within thy frame;
Then let no recreant thought or deed divert thy upward aim

Shall earth's brief ills appall the brave? Shall manly hearts despond?
Tho' darkly now the cloud may frown, the blue heaven sleeps beyond!

II.

Dost inly pine at others' gold?—gay trappings?—dainty fare?
Dost envy Power or titled Rank the homage that they share?
Tho' endless wealth were thine, with lands stretching from pole to pole,
Could all earth's power or pelf atone for poverty of soul?

III.

In faith the patient spirit finds a world-defying spell;
Knowing that, come to it what may, God doeth all things well.
Thus 'mid the roughest ills of life a blest repose it keeps,
Firm as the beacon 'mid the foam the tempest round it heaps.

IV.

Then, brother, trust the immortal life glowing within thy frame;
Never let recreant thought or deed divert thy upward aim.
Undaunted meet earth's fleeting ills—rise, and no more despond!
Up, faint heart, up! the blackest cloud but veils the heaven beyond!

THE RAINBOW.

My heart leaps up when I behold
A rainbow in the sky;
So was it when my life began;
So is it now I am a man;
So be it when I shall grow old,
Or let me die!
The child is father of the man,
And I could wish my days to be
Bound each to each by natural piety.

WORDSWORTH.

LESSON LI.

AL-TER'NATE-LY, by turns.

BRIT'TLE, easily broken; frail.

DAM'ASK, linen woven with figures. (So called from the city of Damascus.)

FI'BROUS, containing fibers.

FRAG'ILE (fraj'il), brittle; weak

THEBES (theebz), once a famous city, the capital of Egypt, on the Nile.

THE FLAX PLANT AND LINEN.

1. THE flax plant, which affords the raw material of the linen manufacture, is a graceful annual, often found growing wild. The stalk is slender, about two feet high, and has small pointed leaves placed alternately on the stem. It bears exceedingly delicate pale blue flowers; but these fragile blossoms soon fade and fall away.

2. The flax plant seems to thrive best in a moist climate. It is largely and successfully cultivated in the north of Ireland. The seeds are sown in March; and the plants, when the seeds are ripe in autumn, are pulled up by the roots. Of the seeds linseed oil is made; and if the object be to save the seeds, the plants are spread out in the sun to dry, but if the fibrous part be the chief object, the plants are tied up in bundles and laid to soak in pools or ponds of water. By this means the pulpy part of the stalk dissolves, and the fibers are loosened.

3. The bundles are then taken out and spread in a sunny place till the stalks are quite brittle, when the fibrous part is easily separated, by beating, from the rest of the plant. After various pro-

cesses of cleaning and combing, it is in a fit state to be spun into thread. The chief textures manufactured from flax are known by the names of *linens, damasks, shirtings*, etc. The coarser and stronger kinds are used for *sail-cloth, sheeting, canvas*, etc. The finest flax texture is *cambric;* so named because it was first manufactured in the town of Cambrai, in the north of France.

4. The art of making fine linen out of flax fibers has been known and practiced for more than four thousand years. Linen was esteemed above woolen cloth in the East, and is mentioned several times in the Scriptures as an indication of the rank of the wearer. In the parable of the Rich Man and Lazarus, we are told only two things about the outward state of the rich man, and they relate to his clothing and his food. He "was clothed in purple and fine linen."

5. These words are quite sufficient to inform us of his riches, even if it were not added that "he fared sumptuously every day;" for the woolen cloth dyed purple was very rare and costly, only worn by kings and great persons; and the "fine linen" was a most choice and expensive material, and to be obtained only by the rich.

6. Linen was, in the earliest period of civilization, the most delicate material for garments. The ancient Egyptians were acquainted with the art of spinning and weaving flax in the time of their greatest prosperity, nearly three thousand years ago. Linen cloth was not only used for garments

by kings and rich subjects in their lifetime, but the mummies found in the royal tombs of the pyramids at Thebes were wrapped in fine linen.

LESSON LII.

AD-JA′CENT, near; close by.
AP-PRO′PRI-ATE, fit; suitable.
CHRYS′A-LIS (kris′-), the gold-colored sheath of butterflies. (From the Greek, *chrusos*, gold.)
CO-COON′, the ball made by the silk-worm.
FIL′A-MENT, a thread.
MAN-U-FACT′URE, (man-yu-fakt′-yur), anything made by art.
MO-NOP′O-LY, sole right of selling or possessing.
O′VAL, shaped like an egg.
TRANS-PAR′ENT, that may be seen through.
VO-RA′-CIOUS-LY, greedily.

THE SILK MANUFACTURE.

1. IN the early part of the sixth century two monks on a mission to China brought away with them a quantity of silk-worm eggs, concealed in a piece of hollow cane, which they carried to Constantinople. There they hatched the eggs, reared the worms, and spun the silk; for the first time introducing that manufacture into Europe, and destroying the monopoly which China had hitherto enjoyed.

2. From Constantinople the knowledge and the practice of the art gradually extended to Greece, thence to Italy, and next to Spain. Each country, as in turn it gained possession of the secret, strove to preserve it with jealous care; but to little purpose. A secret that so many thousands already shared in common could not long be kept. Grad-

ually the manufacture became common in the southern countries of Europe.

3. The silk-worm is the caterpillar of the mulberry tree moth. This tree seems almost exclusively its own; for while other trees and vegetables nourish myriads of insects, the mulberry tree is seldom attacked by any but this insect, which, in many parts of its native country, China, is found on the leaves in the open air.

4. It there goes through all its changes without any attention from man, whose only care is to gather in the harvest of silk cocoons at the right season. In some parts of China, however, the silk-worm requires the same care, in the way of shelter, feeding and nursing, which in other countries is found necessary to insure success.

5. The silk-worm when first hatched is about a quarter of an inch long. If supplied with appropriate food, it remains contentedly in one spot. After eight days' feeding and rapid increase in size, it prepares to change its skin, which has become too small for its body. This operation is facilitated by silken lines which the insect casts off and fixes to adjacent objects; these hold the old skin tightly while the caterpillar creeps out of it.

6. It immediately begins again to eat voraciously, and in five days more another change of skin is necessary. Four of these renewals bring the insect to its full size, which is about three inches long Arrived at maturity, the caterpillar is of a rich golden hue. It then leaves off eating and

selects a corner in which to spin its cocoon. It first forms a loose structure of floss silk, and then within it the closer texture of its nest, which is of an oval shape.

7. Here it remains spinning and working until it is gradually lost sight of within its own beautiful winding-sheet. On the completion of its cocoon it changes its skin once more, and then becomes an apparently inanimate chrysalis, with a smooth brown skin. It remains in this corpse-like state for a fortnight or three weeks, when it comes forth a perfect winged insect—the silk-moth.

8. In escaping from the cocoon, it pushes the fibers aside; having no teeth, it cannot gnaw its way out, as is generally supposed. In the perfect form, the insect takes no food, and only lives two or three days.

9. The silk of the silk-worm is a fine yellow, transparent gum, which hardens as it becomes exposed to the air when issuing from the insect's body. The length of filament yielded by a single cocoon is about three hundred yards. This filament, however, is so fine that it takes upward of two thousand cocoons to make a pound weight of silk.

10. Attempts to breed and rear silk-worms have generally failed in the United States, partly from the unfitness of the climate, and partly from the high rate of wages, which renders this employment better adapted to the social condition of China and the south of Europe.

LESSON LIII.

THE TWO RAIN-DROPS.

I.

SAID a drop to a drop, "Just look at me!
I'm the finest rain-drop you ever did see:
I have lived ten seconds at least on my pane,
Swelling and filling, and swelling again.

II.

"All the little rain-drops unto me run,
I watch them, and catch them, and suck them up each one!
All the pretty children stand and at me stare,
Pointing with their fingers—'That's the biggest drop there!'"

III.

"Ah! yet you are but a drop," the small drop replied;
"I don't myself see any great cause for pride:

The bigger you swell up, we know well, my friend,
The faster you'll run down, the sooner you'll end.

IV.

"For me, I'm contented outside on my ledge,
Hearing the patter of rain in the hedge,
Looking at the fire-light and the children fair;
Whether they look at *me*, I'm sure I don't care."

V.

"Sir," cried the first drop, "your talk is but dull;
I can't wait to listen, for I'm almost full;
You'll run a race with me? No? Then 'tis plain
I am the greatest drop on the whole pane."

VI.

Off ran the big drop, at first rather slow,
Then faster and faster, as drops will, you know:
Raced down the window-pane like hundreds before,
Just reached the window-sill—one splash—and was o'er.

LESSON LIV.

As-so'ci-ate, (-shĭ-) a companion.
Fru-i'tion (froo-ish'un), use accompanied with enjoyment.
In-del'i-ble, not to be effaced.
Man'na, a honey-like juice got from a kind of ash tree found in the south of Europe.
Vi'brate, to quiver.

Avoid saying *ax* for *acts*. Give *o* in *nothing* and *none* the sound of short *u*.

INFLUENCE OF EXAMPLE.

1. Every morning we enter upon a new day that carries an unknown future in its bosom. How stirring the reflection! Thoughts may be born to-day which may never die. Feelings may be awakened to-day which may never be extin-

guished. Hopes may be excited to-day which may never expire. Acts may be performed to-day the consequences of which may not be realized till eternity.

2. No man's acts die utterly. It is a terrible thought to remember that nothing can be forgotten. I have somewhere read that not an oath is uttered that does not continue to vibrate through all time in the wide-spread current of sound—not a prayer lisped that its record is not to be found stamped on the laws of nature by the indelible seal of the Almighty's will.

> "We live in deeds, not years; in thoughts, not breaths;
> In feelings, not in figures on a dial.
> We should count time by heart-throbs. He most lives
> Who thinks most, feels the noblest, acts the best,
> And he whose heart beats quickest lives the longest."

3. Every act we do or word we utter, as well as every act we witness or word we hear, carries with it an influence which not only extends over our whole future life, and gives to it color and direction, but produces some effect, slight or important, upon the whole frame of society. And herein lies the great significance of setting forth a good example —a silent teaching, which even the poorest person and the humblest child can enforce by his daily life.

4. Let us first take heed to our thoughts, for thoughts resolve themselves, sooner or later, into habits and deeds. To think is to live. To-day is

the time for all good resolutions and for all first steps in improvement:

O bright presence of to-day, let me wrestle with thee, gracious angel!
I will not let thee go except thou bless me; bless me, then, to-day!
O sweet garden of to-day, let me gather of thee, precious Eden;
I have stolen bitter knowledge, give me fruits of life to-day.
O true temple of to-day, let me worship in thee, glorious Zion:
I find none other place nor time than where I am to-day.
O living rescue of to-day, let me run into thee, ark of refuge:
I see none other hope nor chance but standeth in to-day.
O rich banquet of to-day, let me feast upon thee, saving manna;
I have none other food nor store but daily bread to-day.

COR'EI (cŏr'ay), the side of the hill where the game lies.
COR'O-NACH (-nak), a dirge.
CUM'BER, trouble; vexation.
FOR'RAY, a sudden attack for plunder; a ravaging.

CORONACH.

HE is gone on the mountain, he is lost to the forest,
Like a summer-dried fountain, when our need was the sorest.
The fount, reappearing, from the rain-drops shall borrow,
But to us comes no cheering, to Duncan no morrow!

The hand of the reaper takes the ears that are hoary,
But the voice of the weeper wails manhood in glory;
The autumn winds, rushing, waft the leaves that are serest,
But our flower was in flushing when blighting was nearest.

Fleet foot on the corei, sage counsel in cumber,
Red hand in the forray, how sound is thy slumber!
Like the dew on the mountain, like the foam on the river,
Like the bubble on the fountain, thou art gone, and for ever!

LESSON LV.

CEIL'ING, the inner roof.	I-DE'A, notion; thought.
DE-VICE', scheme; contrivance.	VI'ANDS, eatables; victuals.

Pronounce *Damocles, dăm'ŏ-kleez; Dionysius, dī-ŏ-nĭs'ĭ-ŭs.* Sicily is a large island in the Mediterranean Sea.

THE KING AND THE FLATTERER.

1. DIONYSIUS, the tyrant of Sicily, was far from being happy, though he had great riches and all the pleasures which wealth could procure. Damocles, one of his flatterers, told him that no monarch had ever been greater or happier than Dionysius. "Hast thou a mind," said the king, "to taste this happiness, and to know what that is of which thou hast so high an idea?" Damocles with joy accepted the offer.

2. The king ordered that a royal banquet should be prepared, and a gilded sofa placed for the flatterer. There were sideboards loaded with gold and silver plate of immense value. Pages of great beauty were ordered to attend his table, and to obey his commands. Fragrant ointments, flowers and perfumes were added to the feast, and the table was spread with choice delicacies of every kind. Damocles, over-elated with pleasure, fancied himself amongst superior beings.

3. But in the midst of all this happiness, as he lies indulging himself in state, he sees let down from the ceiling, just over his head, a large bright sword hung by a single hair. This sight puts an end to his joy. The pomp of his attendance, the glitter of the carved plate and the delicacy of the viands cease to afford him any pleasure. He dreads to stretch forth his hand to the table. He throws off the garland of roses.

4. He hastens to remove from so dangerous a situation, and earnestly begs the king to restore him to his former humble condition, having no desire to enjoy any longer a happiness so terrible. By this device Dionysius showed to Damocles how wretched was he, the king, in the midst of all the treasures and all the honors which royalty could bestow. But because the humbler lot may be the easier, it does not follow that we ought to prefer it Had the king been a good man and a wise ruler, he might have defied the suspended sword so long as he was true to his duty.

LESSON LVI.

AN-NOY', *n.*, disturbance.
BIG'OT, a zealot; a dogmatist.
BOONS, favors granted.
BRAND, a sword; a fire-brand.
EX'QUI-SITE (-zĭt), select: rare.
GALL (gäl), rancor; bitterness.
GOS'SA-MER, *a.*, light; flimsy.
PEERS, equals; mates.
SUP'PLI-ANT, entreating; begging; imploring.

THE THREE WISHES.

I.

THREE schoolfellows once, on a summer day,
Having fairly tired themselves out at play,
Lay down by the bank of a rippling stream
To dream of the future, as young hearts dream,
And to tell to each other, again and again,
The deeds they would do when they should be men.

II.

The First one carelessly lifted his head,
And his dark eye flashed as he proudly said:
"A few short years, and the sound of my name
Shall fill the ringing trumpet of Fame;
I will lead men on to the field afar;
I will come from thence with the spoils of war!
A mighty force will I hold in my hand—
Thousands shall wait on my least command;
The fairest and bravest for me shall live,
Craving the boons that are mine to give;
And the laurel wreath and the sounding lay
And the rush of proud music shall greet my way!"

III.

The Second looked up, and his eyes of blue
Flashed prouder than his of the darker hue;
"Boast of your slaves with the suppliant knee—
You and your peers, bend your souls to *me!*

My life shall be like a beautiful dream:
Like beauty to ashes, to yours it shall seem!
I will send my fancy on gossamer wings
To roam the earth for its loveliest things:
The pen I shall wield with my own right hand
Shall mightier be than your murderous brand;
It shall master the heart with its exquisite skill—
You shall laugh, you shall weep, hope or fear, at my will!'

IV.

With a glance at the bright blue sky above,
The Third said: "Give me but truth and love—
Truth for my mind and love for my heart—
Then, with a will, let me do my part;
Truth that may shed on Error's host
The light that shall conquer Evil most;
Love that may see in the poorest being
The wonderful work of God the all-seeing;
That with tender eye may look upon all,
And spurn from my heart the bigot's gall;
And give of itself and of truth from my store,
And, by every giving, gain all the more!"

V.

I cannot say how these boys turned out:
That is a matter for gravest doubt;
The First may have found that the battle of life
For him was enough of trial and strife;
The Second may, moth-like, have burnt his wings:
Dreaming and doing are different things!
But I know full well that the wish of the Third
Was of all these wishes the least absurd.
What better guides would you have, dear boy,
Than truth and love 'mid the world's annoy?
Pray for them, then, with earnest heart,
And go forth boldly to do thy part!

LESSON LVII.

COM-PET'I-TORS, rivals.
CON-DEN-SA'TION, the act of making more close or compact.
DIS-CON-CERT'ED, abashed.
GARRULOUS (găr'roo-lŭs), talkative.
GENUINE (jĕn'ū-ĭn), real; true.
INTRIGUING (in-treeg'ĭng), plotting.
JAR'GON, confused talk; gabble.
JUDG'MENT, faculty of judging.
LA-CON'IC, short; pithy; concise.
MEM'PHIS (-fis), a city of Egypt.
MAS'TER-PIECE, a capital performance.
OB'VI-OUS, easily perceived; plain.
PAR'SI-MO-NY, stinginess.
PRO-VIN'CIAL, belonging to a province.
SU-PER-NU'MER-A-RY, exceeding the number stated or prescribed.
TREAT'ISE (-ĭs or ĭz), a written composition on a particular subject.
U-NAN'I-MOUS, being of one mind.
VER-BOSE', wordy; prolix.

THE SILENT ACADEMY.

1. IN Memphis, the capital of ancient Egypt, there was a famous academy, one of the rules of

which was as follows: "Members will meditate much, write little and talk the least possible." The institution was known as "The Silent Academy," and there was not a person of any literary note in Egypt who was not ambitious of belonging to it.

2. Akmed, a young Egyptian of great learning and exquisite judgment, was the author of a treatise entitled "The Art of Brevity." It was a masterpiece of condensation and precision, and he was laboring to compress it still more, when he learned, in his provincial seclusion, that there was a place vacant in the Silent Academy.

3. Although he had not yet completed his twenty-third year, and a great number of competitors were intriguing for the place, he went and presented himself as a candidate. A crowd of gossiping loungers on the portico speedily drew near and asked him a great many questions. Without uttering a word in reply, Akmed approached one of the ushers and placed in his hands a letter addressed to the president. It contained these words: "Akmed humbly solicits the vacant place." The usher delivered the letter at once, but Akmed and his application had arrived too late. The place was already filled.

4. By arts which even academies sometimes find irresistible, the favorite candidate of a certain rich man had been elected. The members of the Silent Academy were sorry when they learned what they had lost in consequence. The new member was a glib and garrulous pretender, whose verbose jargon

was as unprofitable as it was wearisome, whereas Akmed, the scourge of all babblers, never gave utterance to an unwise word.

5. How should they communicate to the author of "The Art of Brevity" the bad news of the failure of his application? They were at a loss for the best mode of proceeding, when the president hit upon this expedient: he filled a goblet with water, but so full that a single drop more would have caused it to overflow. Then he made a sign that the candidate should be introduced.

6. Akmed entered the hall where the members were all assembled. With slow and measured steps, and that genuine modesty of demeanor which ever accompanies true merit, he advanced. At his approach the president politely rose and, without uttering a word, pointed out to him, with a gesture of regret, the fatal token of his exclusion. Smiling at the emblem, the meaning of which he at once comprehended, the young Egyptian was not disconcerted. Believing that the admission of a supernumerary member would do no harm, and would violate no essential law of the academy, he picked up a rose leaf which he saw lying at his feet, and placed it on the surface of the water so gently that it floated without causing the slightest drop to overflow.

7. At this apt and obvious reply a general clapping of hands spoke the admiration of the members. By unanimous consent they suspended their rules so as to make an exception in favor of Ak-

med's admission. They handed him their registry of names, and he inscribed his own name at the end. It now only remained for him to pronounce, according to custom, an address of thanks, but he was resolved to act consistently with that principle of the academy which enjoined the utmost parsimony of words.

8. On the margin of the column where he had written his name he traced the number 100, representing his brethren of the academy and the number to which they had been limited. Then placing a cipher before the figure 1 (thus, 0100), he wrote underneath: "Their number has been neither diminished nor increased." Delighted at the laconic ingenuity and becoming modesty of Akmed, the president shook him affectionately by the hand, and then, substituting the figure 1 for the cipher which preceded the number 100 (thus, 1100), he appended these words: "Their number has been increased tenfold."

LESSON LVIII.

AUG-MENT′, to increase.
E-LAPSE′, to pass away.
IM-PET′U-OUS, furious.
PELF, money; lucre.
RAN′SOM, to liberate.
SOD′DEN (sŏd′dn), to stew.
SQUAD′RON (skwŏd′-), a part of an army.

EXERCISES IN EMOTIONAL DELIVERY.

1.—FIDELITY.—*Aaron Hill.*

O MY young friend, be obstinately just;
Indulge no passion and betray no trust.

Let never man be bold enough to say,
Thus, and no farther, shall my passion stray;
The first crime past compels us into more,
And guilt grows *fate* that was but *choice* before.

2.—Death for Freedom.—*Byron.*

They never fail who die
In a great cause! The block may soak their gore,
Their heads may sodden in the sun, their limbs
Be strung to city gates and castle walls,
But still their spirit walks abroad. Though years
Elapse, and others share as dark a doom,
They but augment the deep and sweeping thoughts
That overpower all others, and conduct
The world, at last, to freedom.

3.—Hotspur in Anger.—*Shakespeare.*

He said he would not ransom Mortimer;
Forbade my tongue to speak of Mortimer;
But I will find him when he lies asleep,
And in his ear I'll hollo, *Mortimer!*
Nay, I'll have a starling shall be taught to speak
Nothing but Mortimer, and give it him
To keep his anger still in motion.

4.—Remorse of Macbeth.—*Shakespeare.*

I have lived long enough: my way of life
Is fallen into the sere, the yellow leaf;
And that which should accompany old age,
As honor, love, obedience, troops of friends,
I must not look to have; but, in their stead,
Curses, not loud, but deep—*mouth*-honor—breath!
Which the poor heart would fain deny, but dare not.

5.—Antony on Brutus.—*Shakespeare.*

This was the noblest Roman of them all:
All the conspirators, save only he,

Did that they did in envy of great Cæsar;
He only, in a general honest thought
And common good to all, made one of them.
His life was gentle, and the elements
So mixed in him that Nature might stand up,
And say to all the world, "This was a man!"

6.—Improve the Present.—*Dryden.*

Happy the man, and happy he alone,
He who can call *to-day* his own;
He who, secure within, can say,
To-morrow, do thy worst, for I have lived to-day!
Be fair or foul, or rain or shine,
The joys I *have* possessed in spite of fate are mine.
Not Heaven itself upon the past has power,
But what has been, has been, and I have had my hour.

7.—Battle of Waterloo.—*Byron.*

And there was mounting in hot haste: the steed,
The mustering squadron and the clattering car
Went pouring forward with impetuous speed,
And swiftly forming in the ranks of war;
And the deep thunder, peal on peal, afar,
And near, the beat of the alarming drum,
Roused up the soldier ere the morning star,
While thronged the citizens, with terror dumb,
Or whispering with white lips, "The foe! they come! they come!"

8.—Love of Country.—*Scott.*

Breathes there a man with soul so dead,
Who never to himself hath said,
"This is my own, my native land?"
Whose heart hath ne'er within him burned,
As home his footsteps he hath turned
From wandering on a foreign strand?

If such there breathe, go, mark him well:
For him no minstrel raptures swell!
High though his titles, proud his name,
Boundless his wealth as wish can claim;
Despite those titles, power and pelf,
The wretch, concentered all in self,
Living, shall forfeit fair renown,
And, doubly dying, shall go down
To the vile dust, from whence he sprung,
Unwept, unhonored and unsung.

LESSON LIX.

AN-TAG′O-NISM, opposition.
CON-TEM′PLATE, to meditate.
DE-PART′MENT, a division.
DE-PRE′CI-ATE (de-pre′she-ate), to undervalue; to disparage.
EV-A-NES′CENT, transient.
LAV′ISH-LY, freely; profusely.
PER-PE-TU′I-TY, endless duration
TRAN′SI-TO-RY, quickly vanished.
TRIB′UTE, tax; offering.

NATURE AND ART.*

1. AMONG the greatest errors that language has imposed upon us, there is none more remarkable than the sort of antagonism which is established in common language as between nature and art. We speak of art as being, in a certain manner, the rival of nature and opposed to it; we contrast them —we speak of the superiority of nature, and depreciate art as compared with it. On the other hand, what is art but the effort that is made by human

---

* From an address to workingmen delivered in Manchester, England, in 1857, by Nicholas Wiseman, who was born in Spain of English parents in 1802, and has held a prominent position as a Catholic preacher and writer. He was made a cardinal in 1852.

skill to seize upon the transitory features of nature, to give them the stamp of perpetuity?

2. If we study nature, we see that in her general laws she is unchangeable; the year goes on its course, and day after day the earth passes magnificently through the same revolutions. But there is not one single moment in which either nature, or anything that belongs to her, is stationary. The earth, the planets and the sun and moon are not for any instant in exactly the same relation mutually as they were in a previous instant. The face of nature is constantly changing; and what is it that preserves that for us but art, which is not the rival, but the child, as well as the handmaid, of nature?

3. You find, when you watch the setting sun, how beautiful and how bright it is for an instant, then how it fades away! The sky and sea are covered with darkness, and the departed light is reflected still upon your mind as it had been just now upon the water. In that one evanescent moment a Claude or a Stanfield* dips his pencil in the glowing sky, and transfers its hue to his canvas; and ages after, by the lamp of night, or in the brightness of the morning, we can contemplate that evening scene of nature, and again renew in ourselves all the emotions which the reality could impart.

* Claude Lorraine, a famous Italian landscape painter, died in 1682 Stanfield is a modern English painter of high celebrity.

4. Let us, therefore, look on art but as the highest image that can be made of nature. Consequently, while religion is the greatest and noblest mode in which we acknowledge the magnificent and all-wise majesty of God, and what he has done both for the spiritual and the physical existence of man, let us look upon art as but the most graceful and natural tribute of homage we can pay to him for the beauties which he has so lavishly scattered over creation.

5. Art, then, is a sacred and a reverend thing, and one which must be treated with all nobleness of feeling and with all dignity of aim. We must not depress it; our education in it must always be tending higher and higher; we must fear the possibility of our creating a mere lower class of artists who would degrade the higher departments. Let us rather endeavor to blend and harmonize every department, so that there shall cease to exist in the minds of men the distinction between high and low art.

KNOWLEDGE AND WISDOM.

KNOWLEDGE and wisdom, far from being one,
Have ofttimes no connection. Knowledge dwells
In heads replete with thoughts of other men;
Wisdom, in minds attentive to their own.
Knowledge—a rude, unprofitable mass,
The mere materials with which Wisdom builds,
Till smoothed, and squared, and fitted to its place—
Does but encumber whom it seems to enrich.
Knowledge is proud that he has learned so much:
Wisdom is humble that he knows no more.

LESSON LX.

COM-MEM′O-RAT-ED, celebrated.
FLEET, company of ships.
RES′CUED, saved; brought off.
SHONE (shŏn or shōn), did shine.

THE LITTLE MIDSHIPMAN.

1. THE little midshipman had been told by his father to take a position on the deck, and not to leave it until he ordered him to do so. The midshipman's name was Casabianca, and he was ten years old. He and his father were in the Orient, one of the ships of the French fleet which, in August, 1798, fought the English fleet, under Lord Nelson, in the bay near Alexandria, Egypt.

2. About nine o'clock at night the good ship Orient caught fire, and blazed so brightly that the

bay shone as if it were day. Then Lord Nelson made a signal to his ships that they should stop firing, and ordered his sailors to row in their small boats to the burning vessel and rescue those who still remained on board.

3. The French sailors gladly surrendered, to escape from the wreck, which they knew must blow up as soon as the flames reached the powder-magazine. They therefore hastened to spring into the English boats, but not until they had called to their little favorite, Casabianca, to come with them.

4. Some of the sailors ran to bring him, but he refused to quit his post. They told him that the ship must soon blow up; they entreated him to come with them; but still he answered that he would not leave until his father ordered him to go.

5. In the French reports of the battle it is said that the boy replied, "No, I am where my father stationed me, and I will not move save at his call." Then he was told that his father was wounded and dying, and would never call him again.

6. Still the boy would not go with the sailors, but hastened to render such aid as he could to his father. By the light of the burning ship the sailors, rowing away, saw the brave lad kneeling beside his father's form, and lashing it to the fragment of a mast which had been shot away and had fallen on the deck.

7. He was then seen to drag the mast and his

father's body to the side of the vessel, whence he sprang with his precious charge into the water. Almost at the same instant a fearful explosion, which shook every ship in the harbor, blew the Orient into a thousand pieces. As soon as the flying and burning fragments had fallen, the English boats returned to aid any person who might be struggling in the water.

8. For a moment the crew of one boat saw at a distance the helpless figure of the boy's father bound to the mast, and the little midshipman struggling to keep his head above the waves; but before they could reach the spot, darkness had settled over it; the noble little fellow had sunk, and was never seen again. His heroic conduct has been worthily commemorated by Mrs. Hemans in the following familiar lines:

I.

The boy stood on the burning deck, whence all but him had fled;
The flame that lit the battle's wreck shone round him o'er the dead;
Yet beautiful and bright he stood, as born to rule the storm—
A creature of heroic blood, a proud though child-like form!

II.

The flames rolled on—he would not go without his father's word;
That father, faint in death below, his voice no longer heard.
He called aloud, "Say, father, say if yet my task is done?"
He knew not that the chieftain lay unconscious of his son.

III.

"Speak, father," once again he cried, "if I may yet be gone!"
And but the booming shots replied, and fast the flames rolled on.
Upon his brow he felt their breath, and in his waving hair,
And looked from that lone post of death in still yet brave despair!

IV.

He shouted yet once more aloud, "My father, must I stay?"
While o'er him fast, thro' sail and shroud, the wreathing fires made way.
They wrapped the ship in splendor wild, they caught the flag on high,
And streamed above the gallant child like banners in the sky.

V.

Then came a burst of thunder sound! The boy—oh where was he?
Ask of the winds, that far around with fragments strewed the sea,
With mast and helm and pennon fair, that well had borne their part;
But the noblest thing that perished there was that young faithful heart!

LESSON LXI.

COL-LU'SION (kol-lu'zhun), a secret agreement for fraud.
FEAT, a rare deed; a trick.
FOR'TI-TUDE, endurance.
JUG'GLER, one who practices sleight-of-hand tricks.
STAFF, officers about a general.
SEN'SI-TIVE, having acute feelings.

Pronounce Napier *Na'pe-er;* extraordinary, *eks-tror'di-na-ry.*

NAPIER AND THE JUGGLER.

1. SIR CHARLES NAPIER was an English general of extraordinary courage and determination. He

was born in the year 1782. As a child he was weak and sickly, but of a noble spirit. Bold and fearless, he was at the same time compassionate as a girl. Naturally sensitive, he could, by his force of will, call up daring and fortitude to conquer his timidity.

2. When he became a general he took the right method for inspiring his men with his own heroic spirit. He worked as hard as any private soldier in the ranks. "The great art of commanding," he said, "is to take a fair share of the work. The man who leads an army can not succeed unless his whole mind is given to his task."

3. An anecdote of his interview with a famous Indian juggler shows his cool courage as well as his simplicity and honesty of character. After a certain battle this juggler visited the camp and performed his feats before the general, his family and staff. Among other performances, the man cut in two with a stroke of his sword a lime or lemon placed in the hand of his assistant.

4. Sir Charles thought there was some collusion between the assistant and the juggler. To divide by a sweep of the sword on a man's hand so small an object without touching the flesh, he believed to be impossible. To determine the point, he stretched out his right arm, and offered his own hand for the experiment.

5. The juggler looked attentively at the hand, and said he would not make the trial. "I thought I would find you out!" exclaimed Sir Charles.

"But stop," added the juggler; "let me see your left hand." The left hand was submitted, and the man then said firmly, "If you will hold your arm steady, I will perform the feat."

6. "But why the left hand and not the right?" asked Sir Charles. "Because," replied the juggler, "the right hand is hollow in the center, and there is a risk of cutting off the thumb; the left is high, and the danger will be less." Sir Charles was startled. "I got frightened," he afterward said; "I saw it was an actual feat of delicate swordsmanship.

7. "If I had not abused the man before my staff and challenged him to the trial, I honestly acknowledge I would have retired from the encounter. However, I put the lime on my hand, and held out my arm steadily. The juggler balanced himself, and with a swift stroke cut the lime in two pieces. I felt the edge of the sword on my hand as if a cold thread had been drawn across it."

THE EXAMPLE OF BIRDS.

RING-DOVE! resting serenely calm,
Tell my bosom thy secret balm;
Black-bird! straining thy tuneful throat,
Teach my spirit thy thankful note;
Eagle! cleaving the vaulted sky,
Help my nature to soar as high;
Sky-lark! winging thy way to heaven,
Be thy track to my spirit given.

LESSON LXII.

AL′MOND (ăl′mond *or* ä′mond), a nut.
BEV′ER-AGE, drink; potion.
CLEAN′LI-NESS (klĕn′-), neatness.
DE-RANGE′, (-rānj′), to disorder.
DET-RI-MENT′AL, injurious.
EM-BAR′RASS, to clog; to vex.
E-QUIV′A-LENT, equal.
EX′CRE-TO-RY, throwing off from the body what is useless.
FUNC′TIONS, offices; employments.
PU′TRID, corrupt; rotten.
REQ′UI-SITE (rek′we-zit), a thing necessary.
VEN′TI-LATE, to purify with wind.

RULES FOR HEALTH.

1. FOUR things, above all others, are required for keeping the organic structure of the body in a healthy performance of its functions. These are air, food, exercise and cleanliness, and all must be had under proper regulations.

2. Air is only in a proper state for supporting the organic functions when it has a fifth of oxygen in its composition—that is, when it is in its usual state as found in the atmosphere. In a room which does not communicate freely with the open air we soon reduce the quantity of oxygen: in such circumstances every breath we draw is detrimental to health.

3. Hence, all sitting and sleeping apartments should be large and have the ceiling high, or else should have a constant communication with the open air. Churches, schools, factories and all places where multitudes assemble should be well ventilated. The air, however, is nowhere so wholesome as out of doors, and there, accordingly, every human being should spend a considerable portion of every day.

4. Wholesome food is the second great requisite for health. Of the numerous articles of food, some are not easily digested, as pastry, dried and pickled animal food, oily dishes and fruits, especially those which consist of the kernels of nuts, as filberts, hickory nuts and almonds. These, being likely to derange the stomach and occasion pain, ought to be avoided or only indulged in sparingly.

5. Of the beverages commonly in use all those which contain alcohol, as wine, brandy, gin and whisky, are hurtful to the digestive powers. When a judicious selection of articles of meat and drink has been made, it is still to be remembered that a certain quantity is all that nature demands. If, under the influence of a false appetite, we eat or drink more than is required for sustenance, we overload and embarrass the stomach and prepare for ourselves many serious evils.

6. Moderate exercise is necessary to health. The direct object of supply is to allow of waste. As fast as the body is taking in new substance it is giving off something equivalent, and thus a perpetual freshening flow is kept up. Now, in a state of inactivity, this flow is too languid. A certain animation of mind and a certain exertion of the muscular system are necessary for keeping it up, for the muscles, when exerted under the influence of a willing and sprightly mind, take in fresh substance from the blood.

7. We were designed to *labor*—to earn our bread by the sweat of our brow. We have there-

fore been provided with organs fitted to perform labor. When these organs are used in the way ordained by nature—namely, in the way of moderate exercise—her intention is fulfilled, and health is the consequence. When, from indolence or bad habits, we do not exercise our bodily frames, infirmity and bad health ensue.

8. When, in addition to imperfect exercise, there is a want of pure air, the evil consequences to health are proportionally increased. On the other hand, the mind and body ought not to be exercised above their strength, for by such means either may be so injured that death will be hastened.

9. The fourth requisite for health is cleanliness. Bathing, entire or partial, and frequent and regular changes of apparel, are necessary for the qualification of the skin to perform its excretory function. Not knowing this, or from bad habit, many individuals do not wash themselves sufficiently, and hence not only render their persons less healthy, but become unseemly and disagreeable to others.

10. The cleanness of our clothes, however humble they may be, is equally important, and our apartments should be kept dry and regularly swept and well aired. As with our persons and houses, so with the streets and towns we dwell in; they should be daily cleaned, and no putrid matter or stagnant water be allowed to collect in their vicinity. It is of great importance to form habits of cleanliness in early life. When thus formed, they are scarcely ever after neglected.

LESSON LXIII.

IN-COM-PAT-I-BIL′I-TY, want of agreement.
IN′VA-LID, a sick person.
PET′U-LANT, fretful; peevish.
TINCT′URE, a tinge or shade of color; tint; dye.

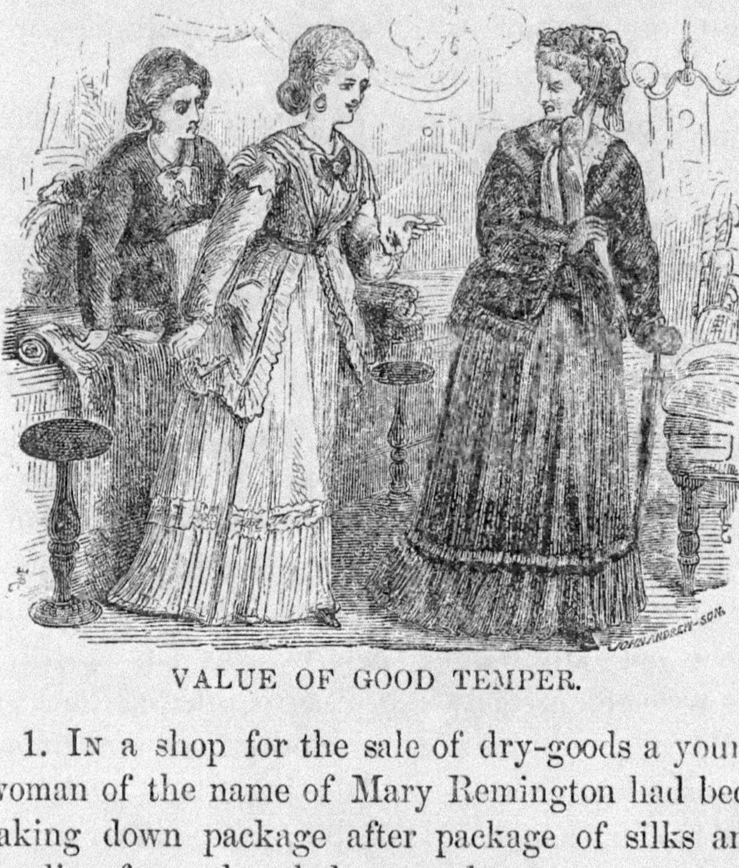

VALUE OF GOOD TEMPER.

1. IN a shop for the sale of dry-goods a young woman of the name of Mary Remington had been taking down package after package of silks and muslins from the shelves, to show to a very particular old lady. For nearly an hour Mary patiently attended to her, and then the old lady remarked, "I think I shall buy nothing to-day."

2. "We shall be glad to have you call again," replied Mary. "I fear I have given you a good deal of trouble," said the old lady. "I would

rather be occupied than stand still," returned Mary, with a smile, which the old lady silently returned, and then left the shop.

3. "How could you be so civil to that old plague?" asked Laura Barclay, who had been standing near. She had come in from an adjoining shop to have a little chat. "Did you ever see her before?" she asked. "Never," replied Mary. "Well," said Laura, "that same old creature came, about an hour ago, into our shop and kept me unrolling goods for her, showing laces and silks, and I don't know what, just as she has been doing here, and wound up in the same way with the remark, 'I think I shall buy nothing to-day.' I couldn't help replying, 'I didn't expect you would.' I let her see what I thought of her."

4. "You did wrong, Laura," said Mary. "You owe it to your employer to treat his customers with perfect patience and respect. Do you know that one reason why shopkeepers object to employing saleswomen instead of salesmen is that their lady customers say they receive more civility from the latter than from the former? You ought to be careful how you give cause for the reproach which our own sex bring against us."

5. The conversation here ended. Laura, petulant and unconvinced, withdrew to her own shop, and Mary turned away to attend to new customers. She went home that night weary and thoughtful. Her mother was a widow and an invalid; there were three younger children in the family, and

they were all dependent for support chiefly on Mary. But she did not long despond.

6. The next day, as she stood at her post behind the counter of the shop, the old lady of the day before entered and made some large purchases. Then turning to Mary, she said: "It was not without a purpose that I troubled you so yesterday." Mary opened her eyes inquiringly. "The truth is," resumed the old lady, "I am in search of a person to take charge of a lace and thread store in our part of the city. We are sadly in want there of such an establishment. I wished to see if you were good-tempered and accommodating; and I was so pleased with the result of the trial that I have concluded to propose that you should take charge of the new shop."

7. Mary was delighted at the prospect; but an objection soon presented itself. "Of course, madam," she said, "it will require money to commence such a business, and that I have not. I am quite poor." "And I am quite rich," retorted the old lady, with a smile; "all the risk shall be mine, and all the profit shall be yours." "But how do you know I am qualified?" asked Mary. "Oh," said the old lady, "I have acquainted myself with your circumstances, habits and capacities. You are a good saleswoman, as I know, a good accountant, as I learn; and, above all, a good daughter. I have seen your mother; she approves. I have seen your employer; he, though reluctant to lose you, gives his consent. Now what say *you?*"

8. To an offer so advantageous Mary could return but one reply. She took possession of the shop, and, aided by the credit of the old lady, stocked the shelves with choice goods. She soon became noted for her exquisite taste in laces. Her gentle and unaffected manners inspired confidence and won hearts. The growth of the city in five years made her shop one of the most central in the principal street. Mary was prosperous beyond her heart's wish, and only labored on for the benefit of others. Her benefactress lived to be proud of the sagacity of her choice. "It was your good temper that won me," she used often to say to Mary.

9. And what became of Laura? Handsome and accomplished, she made what the world called a "brilliant marriage." But there is an old proverb which applies to her case; it is this: "Praise a fair day at night." Laura had not been married five years when she was separated from her husband on the plea of "incompatibility of temper." Poor Laura! She never could learn to give the soft answer which turneth away wrath; and this, in the married state, is a fatal incapacity Indeed, what is the position or relation of life in which good temper is not a treasure and a charm?

"What is the blooming tincture of the skin,
To peace of mind and harmony within?
What the bright sparkling of the finest eye,
To the soft soothing of a calm reply?"

LESSON LXIV.

DIS-EN-CHANT', to free from spells.
RICK'ET-Y, affected with rickets; weak; imperfect.
TIN'SEL, a kind of shining cloth; any thing showy.
TRAP'PINGS, ornaments.

Avoid saying *spere* for *sphere* (*sfere*); *cuss* for *curse; spile* for *spoil; relum* for *rĕalm.* In such words as *helm, elm, chasm,* etc., some speakers have a bad habit of introducing a decided vowel sound before the *m.*

NOTHING TO WEAR.

I.

OH, ladies, dear ladies, the next sunny day
Please trundle your hoops just out of Broadway,
From its whirl and its bustle, its fashion and pride,
And the temples of Trade which tower on each side,
To the alleys and lanes where Misfortune and Guilt
Their children have gathered, *their* city have built;
Where Hunger and Vice, like twin beasts of prey,
  Have hunted their victims to gloom and despair.
Raise the rich, dainty dress, and the fine broidered skirt;
Pick your delicate way through the dampness and dirt;
  Grope through the dark dens, climb the rickety stair
To the garret, where wretches, the young and the old,
Half starved and half naked, lie crouched from the cold!

II.

See those skeleton limbs, those frost-bitten feet,
All bleeding and bruised by the stones of the street;
Hear the sharp cry of childhood, the deep groans that swel
  From the poor dying creature who writhes on the floor;
Hear the curses that sound like Hope's dying farewell,
  As you sicken and shudder and fly from the door;
Then home to your wardrobes, and say, if you dare—
Spoiled children of Fashion—you've nothing to wear!

III.

And oh, if perchance there *should* be a sphere
Where all is made right which so puzzles us here;

Where the glare and the glitter and tinsel of Time
Fade and die in the light of that region sublime;
Where the soul, disenchanted of flesh and of sense,
Unscreened by its trappings, and shows, and pretense,
Must be clothed, for the life and the service above,
With purity, truth, faith, meekness and love,—
O daughters of Earth! foolish virgins, beware!
Lest in that upper realm you have nothing to wear!

FAME.

I.

OH, who shall lightly say that fame
Is nothing but an empty name,
While in that sound there is a charm
The nerves to brace, the heart to warm,
As, thinking of the mighty dead,
  The young from slothful couch shall start,
And yearn, with lifted hands outspread,
  Like them to act a noble part!

II.

Oh, who shall lightly say that fame
Is nothing but an empty name,
When, but for those, our mighty dead,
  All ages past a blank would be,
Sunk in oblivion's murky bed,
  A desert bare, a shipless sea?
They are the distant objects seen,
The lofty marks of what *hath* been.

III.

Oh, who shall lightly say that fame
Is nothing but an empty name,
When memory of the mighty dead,
  To earth-worn pilgrim's wistful eye,
The brightest rays of cheering shed,
  That point to immortality!

LESSON LXV.

FLICK'ER, to waver; to flutter.

PLAN'ET (from a Greek word meaning to wander), a celestial orb.

TUBE, a hollow cylinder; a pipe.

RE-FLECT'ED, thrown back as light, heat, or the like; returned as rays or beams.

THE ASTRONOMER.

1. ASTRONOMY is a word derived from the Greek *astron*, a star, and *nomos*, a law or rule. An astronomer, therefore, is one who studies the laws of the heavenly orbs, their distances and the motions by which they are regulated. It is man,

It is mind, that gives to this great spectacle of the starry heavens all its true worth.

2. While the sun is shining brightly in at my window, I take seven little brass balls and lay them down on the part of the table where the sunshine falls. What do they look like? They are all very bright, and if you look for a moment, you will see a little image of the sun in each of them, just as you see the image of your own face in a looking-glass. But pull down the blind, and what do we see? The balls are not bright now and the little suns have all disappeared, but the sun itself is shining just the same as ever.

3. Well, then, I want you to understand that the sun shines by its own light, but the balls, having no light in themselves, could only shine by giving back the light of the sun. In the same way a blazing fire or a lighted candle shines with its own light, and you may have perhaps observed that the candlestick seemed to shine very brightly too, just as these little balls did. But put out the candle, and you will see that the candlestick will shine no longer, because it has no light in itself, and could only borrow and reflect, or give back, the light thrown upon it by the candle while burning.

4. Now, I wish you to understand the difference between an object shining with its own and with the light of any other bright object shining upon it, which is called reflected light. The sun shines with its own light. The fixed stars shine with

their own light. They are too far from the sun to get much of its light. If I put one of these brass balls down close beside a lighted candle, it may shine brightly enough, but if I put it far away into a dark corner of the room, it will perhaps not shine at all, or at most very dimly.

5. But the fixed stars do not need the sun's light, for they are all suns and have light of their own, though they look smaller than the sun, being so much farther away. The planets, however, do not shine with their own light, but reflect the light of the sun in the same way as the little brass balls did; and the planets keep moving round about the sun, receiving from it both light and heat.

6. Here, then, is another lesson for you to keep in mind: that the principal difference between the fixed stars and the planets is that the former shine with their own light and the latter with light borrowed from the sun. But there is still another difference: the fixed stars, which are very nearly all you can see in the sky on a clear night, are stars that twinkle, but the stars we call planets shine with a steady light, and do not twinkle or flicker like the others.

7. The planets are much nearer to us than the twinkling stars. These last are called *fixed* stars, because they are always seen in nearly the same places, while the planets are constantly changing their places in the sky. There are eleven of these planets; but four of them are smaller than the rest, and two are nearer to the sun than our earth.

LESSON LXVI.

DOR'MANT, sleeping.

PRAI'RIE (prā're), a large natural meadow, or tract of land bare of trees.

SASH, a window-frame.

TOR'PID, numb; sluggish.

VER'MEIL, vermilion.

YEARN, to feel pain or desire.

COME, SUNSHINE, COME!

I.

COME, sunshine, come! thee Nature calls!
  Give to the grape its vermeil hue,
Dispel the frost, the cloud, the storm—
  Come, sunshine, come! the year renew!

II.

The grain lies dormant in the soil,
  The bird sings from the withered tree,
The ice-bound brook, the buried flowers,
  Tarry and watch, and long for thee.

III.

Come, sunshine, come! the torpid Earth
  Beneath thy kisses will awake;
Her blush, her bloom, shall truly tell
  She loves thee for thy own love's sake.

IV.

Lo, at the opened sash, the poor!
  Waiting for thee, their being's sum!
Cold their abode and scant their store—
  Come and relieve them, sunshine, come!

V.

Mountain and vale, and desert waste,
  Prairie and wood, and sea-bound isle,
Herb, tree and insect, roof and spire,
  Kindle to life beneath thy smile.

VI.

Pleasure and love thy coming wait,
  Poets and birds thy coming sing;
Thy quickening kiss creation needs;
  Come, sunshine, come: we yearn for spring!

LESSON LXVII.

A-BYSS′ (ă-bis′), a depth without a bottom; a gulf.

A′RE-A, the surface of any figure or space; any open surface.

BREAK′ERS, waves broken by rocks.

DE-CLIV′I-TY, a slope.

DENSE, thick; compact.

DI′A-MOND or DIA′MOND, the most valuable of all precious stones.

EM′ER-ALD, a precious stone of a green color.

FAN-TAS′TIC, imaginary

TRAV′ERSE, to cross.

NIAGARA AND THE GREAT LAKES.

1. THE most striking feature of North America is the vast chain of lakes which separates Canada

from the territory of the United States. Lake Superior, the greatest of these inland seas, is the largest body of fresh water in the world. It covers an area nearly equal to that of England. Ships of the largest size traverse its waters; and, in violent gales, its waves rise as high as those of the ocean.

2. The four other principal lakes are, Lakes Huron, Michigan, Erie and Ontario, from the last of which issue the surplus waters of the whole, forming the noble river St. Lawrence, which runs an uninterrupted course of seven hundred miles, till it reaches the Atlantic. There is thus a continuous current from the most remote tributary of Lake Superior to the Gulf of St. Lawrence, a distance of more than two thousand miles.

3. All these lakes are now traversed by steam and sailing vessels, which ply in every direction, and, by connecting canals and rivers, are year by year developing the vast resources of the country. Lake Erie and Lake Ontario are united by the river Niagara, the length of which is thirty-three and a half miles. On this river, about twenty miles from Lake Erie, the celebrated falls are situated. They form one of the great wonders of the world, and are, perhaps, the most sublime spectacle the human eye has ever beheld. Here an immense river, after receiving the surplus waters of four vast lakes, thunders in a sea-like flood over a lofty precipice into the abyss beneath.

4. When the Niagara issues from Lake Erie, it

flows tranquilly along, bordered by beautiful banks, till within a mile of the falls. There the water begins to ripple; and a little farther on it breaks into a series of dashing and foaming rapids, as if leaping and rejoicing in the prospect of its approaching majestic plunge. The stream then becomes more tranquil, though rolling with prodigious rapidity, till at last it reaches the brink of the great precipice. Then comes the awful plunge.

5. It is the spectacle of a falling sea. The eye is filled almost to its utmost reach by the rushing of the mighty flood: clouds of spray occupy the atmosphere; and, above all, the tremendous roar of the clashing waters is heard filling the vault of heaven.

6. The fall itself is divided into two unequal portions by a piece of land called Goat Island. The American Fall, on the one side of Goat Island, is one hundred and sixty-four feet high; but the Canadian or Horse-shoe Fall is semicircular in form, and the grander of the two.

7. Its breadth is two thousand feet, and its height one hundred and fifty feet. It falls in one dense mass of green water, calm, unbroken, resistless; though at the edges it separates into drops, which fall like a shower of diamonds sparkling in the sun, and at times so lightly as to be driven up again by the current of air ascending from the deep below, where all is agitation and foam.

8. Looked at from below, the scene is sublime,

strange and awful. The mighty river comes tumbling over the brow of a hill; and, as you look up to it, it seems as if rushing to overwhelm you; then meeting with the rocks as it pours down the declivity, it boils and frets like ocean breakers.

9. Huge mounds of water, smooth, transparent and gleaming like an emerald, rise up and bound over some impediment, then break into silver foam, which leaps into the air in the most graceful and fantastic forms. A little below the falls, the Niagara resumes its usual soft and gentle beauty. The banks are high and beautifully wooded, and the river flows along in its course to Lake Ontario, grandly and tranquilly.

LESSON LXVIII.

IN-EX′O-RA-BLE, unrelenting.
RE-DOUBT′ (re-dout′), an outwork; a fortress.
RE-DRESS′, remedy; relief.
RE-TAL-I-A′TION, the return of like for like; revenge; requital.

NOBLE REVENGE.

1. A YOUNG officer had so far forgotten himself, in a moment of irritation, as to strike a private soldier full of personal dignity and distinguished for his courage. The inexorable laws of military discipline forbade to the injured soldier any redress—he could look for no retaliation by acts. Words only were at his command, and, in a tumult of indignation, as he turned away, the soldier said to his officer that he would "make him repent it."

2. This, wearing the shape of a menace, natu-

rally rekindled the officer's anger, and intercepted any disposition which might be rising within him toward a sentiment of remorse; and thus the irritation between the two young men grew hotter than before.

3. Some weeks after this a partial action took place with the enemy. Suppose yourself a spectator, and looking down into a valley occupied by the two armies. They are facing each other, you see, in martial array. But it is no more than a skirmish which is going on; in the course of which, however, an occasion suddenly arises for a desperate service. A redoubt, which has fallen into the enemy's hand, must be recaptured at any price, and under circumstances of all but hopeless difficulty.

4. A strong party has volunteered for the service; there is a cry for somebody to head them; you see a soldier step out from the ranks to assume this dangerous leadership. The party moves rapidly forward; in a few minutes it is swallowed up from your eyes in clouds of smoke; for one half hour, from behind these clouds, you receive visible reports of bloody strife—fierce repeating signals, flashes from the guns, rolling musketry, and exulting hurrahs, advancing or receding, slackening or redoubling.

5. At length all is over; the redoubt has been recovered; that which was lost is found again; the jewel which had been made captive is ransomed with blood. Crimsoned with glorious gore,

the wreck of the conquering party is relieved and at liberty to return. From the river you see it ascending.

6. The plume-crested officer in command rushes forward, with his left hand raising his hat in homage to the blackened fragments of what was once a flag, whilst with his right hand he seizes that of the leader, though no more than a private from the ranks. *That* perplexes you not; mystery you see none in *that;* for distinctions of order perish, ranks are confounded, "high and low" are words without a meaning, and to wreck goes every notion or feeling that divides the noble from the noble, or the brave man from the brave.

7. But wherefore is it that now, when suddenly they wheel into mutual recognition, suddenly they pause? This soldier, this officer—who are they? Oh, reader, once before they had stood face to face—the soldier that was struck, the officer that struck him. Once again they are meeting, and the gaze of armies is upon them. If for a moment a doubt divides them, in a moment the doubt has perished. One glance exchanged between them publishes the forgiveness that is sealed for ever.

8. As one who recovers a brother whom he has accounted dead, the officer sprang forward, threw his arms around the neck of the soldier, and kissed him, as if he were some martyr glorified by that shadow of death from which he was returning; whilst, on his part, the soldier, stepping back, and carrying his open hand through the beautiful mo-

tions of the military salute to a superior, makes this immortal answer—that answer which shut up forever the memory of the indignity offered to him, even while for the last time alluding to it—"Sir," he said, "I told you before that I would make you repent it!"

LESSON LXIX.

CONJURE (kŭn′jŭr), to raise by magic arts.

COR-RE-SPOND′ENCE, letters.

CUT′LER-Y, edged instruments of steel.

EX-PLOITS′, heroic or daring deeds.

LO′CO-MO′-TIVE, moving from place to place.

PAT′RI-MO-NY, an estate held by inheritance.

PHO′TO-GRAPH (grăf), a drawing produced by the action of light.

WHAT A COMMON MAN MAY SAY.

1. I AM lodged in a house that affords me conveniences and comforts which even a king could

not command some centuries ago. There are ships crossing the seas in every direction, some propelled by steam and some by the wind, to bring what is useful to me from all parts of the earth.

2. In China men are gathering the tea-leaf for me; in the Southern States they are planting cotton for me; in the West India Islands and in Brazil they are raising my sugar and my coffee; in Italy they are feeding silk-worms for me; at home they are shearing sheep to make me clothing; powerful steam-engines are spinning and weaving for me, and making cutlery for me, and pumping the mines that minerals useful to me may be procured.

3. My patrimony was small, yet I have locomotive engines running day and night on all railroads to carry my correspondence. I have canals to bring the coal for my winter fire. Then I have telegraphic lines which tell me what has happened many thousand miles off, the same day of its occurrence; which flash a message for me in a minute to the bedside of a sick relative hundreds of miles distant.

4. And I have editors and printers who daily send me an account of what is going on throughout the world amongst all these people who serve me. By the photograph I procure in a few seconds, at a small expense, a perfect likeness of myself or friend, drawn without human touch by the simple agency of light. And, then, in a corner of my house I have *books!*—the miracle of all my possessions, more wonderful than the wishing cap of the

Arabian tales, for they transport me instantly not only to all places, but to all times.

5. By my books I can conjure up before me to vivid existence all the great and good men of old, and for my own private satisfaction I can make them act over again the most renowned of all their exploits. In a word, from the equator to the pole, and from the beginning of time until now, by my books I can be where I please.

6. This picture is not overcharged, and might be much extended; such being the miracle of God's goodness and providence that each individual of the civilized millions that cover the earth may have nearly the same enjoyments as if he were the single lord of all!

LESSON LXX.

Ecs-tat'ic, rapturous.
La'va (lā'va), liquid matter discharged by volcanoes.
Mart, a market.
Serf'dom, state of slavery.
Sor'did, base; niggardly.

UNCROWNED KINGS.

I.

O ye uncrowned but kingly kings!
Made royal by the brain and heart;
Of all earth's wealth the noblest part,
Yet reckoned nothing in the mart
Where men know naught but sordid things—
All hail to you, most kingly kings!

II.

O ye uncrowned but kingly kings!
Whose breath and words of living flame

Have waked slaved nations from their shame
And bid them rise in manhood's name,
Swift as the curved bow backward springs,
To follow you, most kingly kings!

III.

O ye uncrowned but kingly kings!
Whose strong right arm hath oft been bared
Where fires of righteous battle glared,
And where all odds of wrong ye dared!
To think on you the heart upsprings,
O ye uncrowned but kingly kings!

IV.

O ye uncrowned but kingly kings!
Whose burning songs, like lava poured,
Have smitten like a two-edged sword
Sent forth by heaven's avenging Lord
To purge the earth, where serfdom clings
To all but you, O kingly kings!

V.

O ye uncrowned but kingly kings!
To whose ecstatic gaze alone
The beautiful by heaven is shown,
And who have made it all your own;
Your lavish hand around us flings
Earth's richest wreaths, O noble kings!

VI.

O ye uncrowned but kingly kings!
The heart leaps wildly at your thought,
And the brain fires as if it caught
Shreds of your mantle: ye have fought
Not vainly, if your glory brings
A lingering light to earth, O kings!

LESSON LXXI.

AM′BUSH, a lying in wait for.
ES′CORT, safeguard on a journey.
IN-TER-CEDE′, to plead in favor of.
MAS′SA-CRE (-ker), slaughter.
RE-VOKED′, called back.
WHOOP (hoop), a shout of pursuit

CAPTAIN JOHN SMITH.

1. BORN in England in the year 1579, John Smith entered while yet young upon a life of adventure. Before he was thirty years old he had founded the colony of Jamestown in Virginia.

2. Some seven years afterward, having returned to England, he set sail once more for America, and examined the coast of that region to which he was first to give the name of New England. He discovered the Isles of Shoals off the coast of New

Hampshire; a small monument on one of the islands still records his visit.

3. He gave the name of Cape Ann to the northernmost cape of Massachusetts. Having landed with his men on Eastern Point, a neck of land which helps to form what is now the town of Gloucester, he passed some time there for the purpose of recruiting and taking in fresh water.

4. But it was in Virginia, which region he visited in the spring of 1607, that Smith met with his most surprising adventures. He became the leading man in the colony which he founded on the banks of the James River, and here he had many narrow escapes from the attacks of hostile Indians.

5. On one occasion he was going through a forest with an Indian guide, when the latter uttered the well-known war-whoop. Smith seized him and held him fast, and, at the same instant, an arrow struck Smith on the thigh, but without force enough to harm him much. He soon found he was in the midst of an ambush of Indians, and looking up, saw two bows bent to discharge their arrows at him. Taking the pistols from his belt, he fired several shots which kept the enemy in check, but soon a large number of Indians pressed upon him, and in trying to keep them at bay he stumbled and was overpowered.

6. Smith was conducted before Powhatan, the great Indian chief. A council was held, and it was resolved that the white man should die. The

chief was about to give the fatal signal, when out from a silent group of women ran a girl, not more than twelve years old, who rushed toward the doomed and prostrate prisoner. More quickly than the incident can be described she sprang forward between the uplifted clubs of the executioners and the head of their intended victim. She knelt upon the ground by his side and shielded him affectionately with her arms.

7. At so unexpected an event there was an outcry of wonder from the savage multitude. All looked eagerly to see who the damsel was that had taken so strange an interest in the prisoner, and had so boldly presumed to interfere. They saw that it was Pocahontas, the beloved daughter of their chief. He was so fond of his little girl that he always found it very hard to refuse any request she earnestly urged, and now, when she begged for the white man's life, and pleaded with tears in her eyes that he might be saved, the great chief, as well as his companions, felt disposed to let her have her way. Her prayer for mercy was granted.

8. The sentence of death was revoked. Smith was raised from the ground, released from his bonds, and presented as a slave to the maiden whose timely interposition had saved his life. From that day forward he was to belong to her, to go where she sent him and to obey her wishes in everything. But the chief, supposing that Pocahontas must have been impelled by some spiritual power to rescue Smith, adopted him as his son, took him into his family,

and at last sent him back to Jamestown under an escort.

9. Here Smith soon had an opportunity of requiting Pocahontas for her generous conduct. The white men had captured several Indians. The chief sent his favorite daughter to intercede with Smith for their release. Smith could refuse all other petitioners, but not Pocahontas. He granted her request. He subsequently owed his life a second time to her good offices. She warned him and his party of an intended massacre by the Indians, and her warning was so seasonable that the white men all escaped.

10. In the year 1609 Smith quitted the shores of Virginia for ever. He returned to England, wrote books, and in 1614 sailed again for America. Returning to England, he died there at the age of fifty-two. As for Pocahontas, she married John Rolfe, a young Englishman. With him she visited England, where she received great attention. Her conduct as a wife and mother was worthy of all praise.

THE PLACE TO DIE.

DEATH is a common friend or foe, as different men may hold,
And at its summons each must go, the timid and the bold;
But when the spirit, free and warm, deserts it, as it must,
What matter where the lifeless form dissolves again to dust?

'Twere sweet, indeed, to close our eyes with those we cherish near,
And, wafted upward by their sighs, soar to some calmer sphere;
But whether on the scaffold high, or in the battle's van,
The fittest place where man can die is where he dies for man!

LESSON LXXII.

CAR′BON, pure charcoal.
COM-BUS′TI-BLE, that may burn or be burnt.
CRUDE, raw; coarse; unripe.
DEN′SI-TY, thickness; closeness.
KILNS (kilz), stoves or furnaces.
MAL′LE-A-BLE, ductile; that may be flattened or drawn out by being beaten with a hammer.
ME-TE-OR′-IC, relating to meteors.
SAT′U-RAT-ED (-rāt-), filled full.
UL′TI-MATE-LY, finally.

IRON.

1. THE splendid color of gold, its great density, its imperishable nature and its comparative scarcity have obtained for it the epithet of *precious*, although, in point of utility to man, iron has far higher and more numerous claims to such a title.

2. The innumerable applications of iron in our own day result from the various useful properties of this metal. It can be brought to a fluid state, and made to assume whatever form has been given to the mold designed to receive it; it can be drawn out into bars of any degree of strength, or into wires of any degree of fineness; it can be spread out into plates or sheets; it can be twisted and bent in all directions; it can be made hard or soft, sharp or blunt.

3. Iron may be regarded as the parent of agriculture and of the useful arts, for without it the plowshare could not have rendered the earth fertile. Iron furnishes the scythe and the pruning-hook, as well as the sword and the cannon: it forms the chisel, the needle and the graver; springs of various kinds, from the spring of a watch to that

of a carriage; the chain, the anchor and the compass;—all owe their origin to this most useful of all the metals.

4. We can scarcely move without meeting with new and surprising proofs of the fact that we are indeed living in the age of iron. We travel on land by iron railroads, drawn by engines of iron; we pass over bridges constructed of iron, and often suspended by iron rods; our steamboats are of iron; our pens are of iron; our bedsteads, chairs, stools, and ornaments are frequently of iron; clumsy wooden gates are being superseded by light and elegant structures of iron; buildings of all kinds are supported on pillars of iron, and, to crown all, we build dwelling-houses and light-houses of iron, and transport them to the most distant parts of the globe.

5. Iron is more extensively diffused throughout the crust of the earth than any other metal, and its importance is equal to its abundance, for there is no other substance which possesses so many valuable properties, or is so well adapted to form the instruments which have assisted to bring about, and still continue to maintain, the dominion of mind over matter.

6. Iron in a purely metallic form is of rare occurrence, though in different parts of the world several large masses of metallic iron are known to exist, and other similar masses have at various times been observed to fall from the atmosphere. In South America there is a mass of meteoric iron

estimated at thirty-six thousand pounds' weight, and one in Siberia of sixteen thousand pounds'.

7. The first process in the manufacture of iron is roasting the ore, which is done in kilns or furnaces, or in large heaps in the open air. The effect of roasting the ore is to drive off the water, sulphur and arsenic which it generally contains. It is then mixed with limestone and coke and brought to the blast furnace, which is the most important feature in an iron-work, rising to the height of from fifty to seventy feet, and at times lighting up the country around like a small volcano.

8. The coke, ironstone and limestone ultimately form two liquid products at the bottom of the furnace. One of these is glass, composed of the limestone in combination with the earthy impurities of the ore. This, when drawn off and left to cool, forms *slag* or *cinder*. The other product is liquid iron, combined with the carbon of the fuel.

9. As the materials gradually descend from the top to the bottom of the furnace, the ore, being thus for several hours in contact with the burning fuel, is almost saturated with carbon when it reaches the lower or hottest part of the furnace. Here the melted iron is drawn off at intervals of from eight to twelve hours. This work is continued with double sets of attendants day and night, without intermission, for two or three years, for if the furnace were allowed to cool, the contents would become solid and the furnace be ruined.

10. Previous to each *cast*, a channel, called the

sow, is formed in a bed of sand in front of the furnace. Branching off from the sow, at right angles to it, are a number of smaller channels, called *pigs*. Into these the melted metal is run. The bars when cooled are in the state known commercially as *pig iron*. The general name of the metal in this state is *cast iron*.

11. Iron is employed in the arts in three different states: as *crude* or *cast iron*, as *steel*, and as *wrought iron*, the difference depending upon the relative amount of carbon with which the metal is combined. Cast iron contains a larger proportion of carbon than steel, and steel more than wrought or malleable iron, the best malleable iron having only a very minute portion of carbon. The presence of carbon in cast iron renders the metal more fluid when melted, and, consequently, better suited for casting in molds.

12. When converted into ordinary machinery, cast iron originally worth $5 becomes worth about $20; into large ornamental work, $225; into buckles and Berlin work, $3000, and into buttons, $25,000. A bar of wrought iron, originally worth $5, becomes worth about $12 when worked into horse-shoes; $150 when made into table-knives; $350 when turned into needles; $3250 when in the form of penknife blades; and, to crown all, it becomes worth $250,000 when manufactured into watch-springs. It is susceptible of a high polish. It is combustible when minutely divided, as in the state of filings.

LESSON LXXIII.

DELLS, shady hollows.
FELLS, barren or stony hills.
HEATH'Y, full of heath, a shrub that bears a flower.
IN-TENSE', close; ardent.
LEAGUE (leag), the length of three miles.
SHONE (shŏn *or* shōn), did shine.

LITTLE CHILDREN.

I.

SPORTING through the forest wide;
Playing by the water's side;
Wandering o'er the heathy fells;
Down within the woodland dells;
All among the mountains wild,
Dwelleth many a little child.
Wheresoe'er a foot hath gone,
Wheresoe'er the sun hath shone
On a league of peopled ground,
Little children may be found.

II.

Blessings on them! they in me
Move a kindly sympathy,
With their wishes, hopes and fears,
With their laughter and their tears,
With their wonder so intense
And their small experience.

III.

Little children, not alone
On the wide earth are ye known,
'Mid its labors and its cares,
'Mid its sufferings and its snares!
Free from sorrow, free from strife,
In the world of love and life,
Where no sinful thing hath trod,
In the presence of your God,
Spotless, blameless, glorified,
Little children, ye abide.

LESSON LXXIV.

CO-LOS'SAL (from Colossus, a gigantic statue), huge in size.

CON-VEN'TION, an assembly.

COR'RI-DOR, a passage; a gallery.

COV'E-NANT (kŭv'e-nant), a mutual agreement.

DES'POT, an absolute sovereign.

GUIL'LO-TINE (ghil'lo-teen), a machine for beheading persons.

I-RON'I-CAL, spoken in irony or sarcastic praise.

PRO-SCRIBED', doomed; outlawed.

In *Ro-land'* accent the last syllable; pronounce sacrificed *sak'ri-fizd.*

LAST DAYS OF MADAME ROLAND.

1. DURING the Reign of Terror in France, Madame Roland was brought before the Convention on an absurd charge of treasonable correspondence with England. By her presence

of mind, her acuteness and her wit she baffled and mortified her accusers. But on the 31st of May, 1793, she was again arrested and sent to prison. As an officer was conducting her, he asked if she wished to have the windows of the carriage closed. "No," replied she; "oppressed innocence should not take the attitude of crime and shame. I do not fear the looks of honest men, and I brave those of my enemies."

2. The cowards and ruffians who then had control of public affairs in France were afraid of the talents and the influence of this woman. They determined on her death. They gave her a trial, but it was a mere mockery of justice, a solemn farce. In her address before the Revolutionary Tribunal on the 8th of November, 1793, she spoke as follows:

3. "Not to its own times merely does the generous mind feel that it belongs. It comprehends in its regard the whole human race, and extends its care even to posterity. It was my lot to be the friend of men proscribed and sacrificed by those who hated them for their superiority. And I must perish in my turn! I have a double claim to death at your hands. When Innocence walks to the scaffold at the command of Error and of Guilt, every step she takes is an advance to glory. Might I be the last victim of that furious spirit of party by which you are impelled, with what joy would I quit this unfortunate earth, which swallows up the friends of virtue and drinks the blood of the just!

4. "Truth! Friendship! Country!—sacred ob-

jects, sentiments dear to my heart—accept my last sacrifice! My life was devoted to you, and you will render my death easy and glorious. Righteous Heaven, enlighten this wretched people for whom I invoke liberty! Liberty? Ah! that is for noble minds, not for weak beings who enter into a covenant with guilt, and try to varnish cowardice and selfishness with the name of prudence—not for corrupt wretches who rise from the bed of vice, or from the mire of indigence, to feast their eyes on the noble blood that streams from the scaffold.

5. "Oh no! liberty is the portion of a people who delight in humanity, who revere justice, despise flattery and venerate truth. While you are *not* such a people, O my fellow-citizens, in vain will you talk of liberty. Instead of liberty you will have licentiousness, and to that you will all in your turns fall victims. You will ask for bread, and will get—dead bodies! And at length you will bow down your necks to the yoke, and find your vile refuge in the rule of a despot.

6. "I make no concealment of my sympathies, my opinions. I know that a Roman mother once was sent to the scaffold for lamenting the death of her son. I know that, in times of delusion and party rage, he who dares avow himself the friend of the proscribed exposes himself to their fate. But I do not fear death. I never feared any thing but guilt, and I will not purchase life at the price of a lie. Woe to the times! Woe to the people

among whom to do homage to disregarded truth is to incur their hate! Happy he who, under such circumstances, is bold enough to defy that hate, as I do!"

7. All the eloquence, all the courage, all the feminine beauty, of Madame Roland could not save her from the guillotine. She heard herself sentenced to death with the air of one who saw in her condemnation merely her title to immortality. She rose, and slightly bowing to her craven judges, said, with an ironical smile, "I thank you for considering me worthy to share the fate of the good and great men you have murdered." As she passed along the corridor, where the other prisoners had assembled to greet her return, she looked at them smilingly, and drawing her right hand across her throat, made a sign expressive of cutting off a head. This was her only farewell; it was tragic as her destiny, joyous as her deliverance, and well was it understood by those who saw it.

8. To the last moment did this remarkable woman preserve her presence of mind, her intrepidity, and even her gayety. A colossal statue of Liberty, composed of clay, like the liberty of the time, stood near the scaffold. Bowing before this statue, as though to do homage to a power for whom she was about to die, she exclaimed, "O Liberty, Liberty! how many crimes are committed in thy name!" She then resigned herself to the hands of the executioner, and in a few seconds her head fell into the basket placed to receive it.

YUSSOUF.

I.

A STRANGER came one night to Yussouf's tent,
Saying, "Behold one outcast and in dread,
Against whose life the bow of power is bent,
Who flies, and hath not where to lay his head;
I come to thee for shelter and for food,—
To Yussouf, called through all our tribes, *The Good.*"

II.

"This tent is mine," said Yussouf, "but no more
Than it is God's; come in, and be at peace;
Freely shalt thou partake of all my store
As I of His who buildeth over these
Our tents his glorious roof of night and day,
And at whose door none ever yet heard Nay."

III.

So Yussouf entertained his guest that night,
And, waking him ere day, said, "Here is gold;
My swiftest horse is saddled for thy flight;
Depart before the prying day grow bold."
As one lamp lights another, nor grows less,
So nobleness enkindleth nobleness.

IV.

That inward light the stranger's face made grand,
Which shines from all self-conquest; kneeling low,
He bowed his forehead upon Yussouf's hand,
Sobbing: "O sheik, I cannot leave thee so;
I will repay thee; all this thou hast done
Unto that Ibrahim who slew thy son!"

V.

"Take thrice the gold," said Yussouf, "for with thee
Into the desert, never to return,
My one black thought shall ride away from me;
First-born! for whom by day and night I yearn,
Balanced and just are all of God's decrees!
Thou art avenged: my first-born, sleep in peace!"

LESSON LXXV.

A-NON′, soon; quickly.
A-STERN′, behind the stern.
HAR′AS-SES (hăr′-), wearies; frets.
IM-PET-U-OS′I-TY, violence.
MUS′CU-LAR, full of muscle.
OF′FAL, waste meat; carrion.

Pronounce *Montreal, mŏnt-re-awl′; apparent, ăp-pâre′ent.*

THE SAILOR AND THE ALBATROSS.

1. THE albatross is a web-footed bird of large size that frequents the Southern Ocean, and is seen in the neighborhood of Cape Horn. It often weighs upward of twenty pounds, measuring in its extent of wing from ten to eleven feet, and sometimes even more. It varies in color according to age and season, but is generally more or less tinged with gray on the upper part of the body, the rest of the plumage being white.

2. At sea, its vast extent of wing, its graceful movements, its power displayed in the tempest, when the wind lashes the waves into foam, have excited the admiration of voyagers. Now, high in air, it sweeps in wide circles, anon it descends with the utmost impetuosity, plunges into the water, and, instantly rising, soars aloft with its finny prey. It harasses the flying-fish, or sails round the vessel and picks up the offal thrown overboard. It rises and descends, as if some concealed power guided its motions, without any apparent exertion of muscular energy, and it breasts the gale or mounts high above the stormy vapor with prodigious power and a lordly ease.

3. The albatross will follow a ship for weeks. An instance is told of an albatross which, having been caught and marked with a red ribbon about its leg, and then released, flew three thousand miles in company with a vessel before it left her. This bird must have been on the wing nearly all the time for that vast distance.

4. A remarkable but well-attested story was recently communicated by an officer of the eighty-third British regiment in India to a friend in Montreal. While the division to which the officer belonged was on its way to India, being at the time a short distance eastward of Cape Horn, one of the men was severely flogged for some slight offense. Maddened at the punishment, the poor fellow was no sooner released than, in the sight of all his comrades and the ship's crew, he sprang overboard.

5. There was a high sea running at the time, and, as the man was swept on astern, all hope of saving him seemed to vanish. He struggled with the waves, as if, the moment he found himself in the water, the desire for life had overcome his sudden frenzy. There seemed no possibility of rescue, when all at once an albatross was seen to poise itself over the soldier, and then to make a bold, smooth swoop toward him.

6. What was the amazement of the crowd of spectators on deck on discovering that the drowning soldier had caught hold of the bird! He kept his hold firmly, and the power of the bird was sufficient to sustain him afloat till a boat from the vessel was lowered and rowed to his rescue.

7. But for the assistance thus afforded by the bird, no power on earth could have saved the soldier, as, in consequence of the tremendous sea running, a long time elapsed before the boat could be manned and got down, and all this time the man was clinging to the albatross, whose flutterings and struggles to escape bore him up.

8. Who after this should despair? A raging sea—a drowning man—an albatross!—what eye could see safety under such circumstances? or can we venture to call this chance? Is it not rather a lesson intended to stimulate faith and hope and teach us never to despair, since, in the darkest moment, when the waves dash and the winds roar, and a gulf seems closing over our heads, *there may be an albatross near?*

CPSIA information can be obtained
at www.ICGtesting.com
Printed in the USA
LVHW040009040323
740881LV00003B/344

9 783382 114848